Fifteen
and Falling

SUSAN HOLLIDAY

To dear Alice
with love
and many thanks
for your enduring
friendship.

Susan 25·11·2012

Fifteen and Falling

Susan Holliday

Pollinger Limited

PIP
POLLINGER IN PRINT

Pollinger Limited
9 Staple Inn
Holborn
LONDON
WC1V 7QH

www.pollingerltd.com

First published in Great Britain by Pollinger in Print 2012
in paperback and ebook

A CIP catalogue record is available from the British Library

ISBN paperback: 978-1-905665-79-2
ISBN ePub ebook: 978-1-905665-80-8
ISBN Kindle ebook: 978-1-905665-81-5
ISBN PDF ebook: 978-1-905665-82-2

To Julie, with love.

CONTENTS

A TIME FOR RUNNING

It's a lonely journey on the road,
no stopping with this load,
feet are aching and your body's sore
there's no running any more.
And your heart says it's enough,
winter time and the living's rough,
when your bed's just a wooden floor
there's no running any more.

But I'll be running through the wind and rain,
going there and back again.
Don't go asking where I'll roam,
'cos I've got no home.

Call me up, I'll say I'm fine
be around, I've got the time,
count the cost, tell me the score,
there's no running any more.
Palm to palm we were as one,
without words we'd just begun,
my soul's hungry, my soul is raw,
there's no running any more.

But I'll be running through the wind and rain,
going there and back again.
Don't go asking where I'll roam,
'cos I've got no home.

Where is love if it's rented out,
where is hope if it's full of doubt,
freedom's more than an open door,
there's no running any more.
You're my friend and I won't betray,
memories last till the end of day,
I won't leave like I did before,
there's no running any more.

But I'll be running through the wind and rain,
going there and back again.
Don't go asking where I'll roam,
cos I've got no home.

Mandy Pannett

Part one

Lonely Journey

Chapter one

Where is love?

Sara sat on the little flint wall at the end of her garden and looked out on the fields and downs. Is this love, she wondered, this overwhelming need to see a person and to follow him around? She couldn't make up her mind. She knew it wasn't just the sex thing, though Liam was quite attractive with his dark, wispy hair, pale face and black stubble. No! It was other things like his story telling, the way he drew her in because he wanted her to know what had happened to him, where he had come from. Sometimes she wrote down Liam's stories in a drawing book and hid it in her clothes drawer underneath her diary. Then there were his eyes; they mesmerised her, almond shaped, green as a cat's, flecked with broken up black pieces. Sometimes Liam's eyes were bright and dilated as if another world was inside them. When she dreamed of him, it was his eyes she saw, disembodied, beckoning.

Sara shook back her long hair. Above all he gave her a sense of importance that no-one else gave her nowadays, least of all Mum who wanted to keep her young and protected as if she wasn't four months off sixteen. It drove her mad the way Mum was afraid of everything and went on trying to look after her as if she was nine like Emily. Mum's attitude had started a long time ago, two years and three months, to be precise, the moment Dad had died.

She would never forget that last conversation with her father, it was always flashing into her mind. Mum was out of the ward getting a cup of tea and Dad was lying with his head propped up by two pillows. His thin, thin body was resting still as a statue under a white sheet.

His voice was hoarse. 'Don't be sad, darling, I'll always love you wherever you are.'

She had smiled even though grief filled her body. 'You mean

whatever happens?' She gave him the card she had made. On it she had drawn roses and washed them over with a glaze of watercolours, red, pink and yellow. She had carefully written, in her best calligraphic hand, 'Love you always.'

Her father smiled at her. 'It's beautiful, and, yes darling, I mean whatever happens. Just one thing, keep up with your drawing, won't you? And keep up with Ruby. It's not everyone who has a best friend.' His voice faltered and he closed his eyes. Sara propped the card up on the side locker beside the jug of water and the unopened book. She waited for him to open his eyes and to smile at her again. But he never did.

The flashback floated away and Sara turned round and saw her mother coming out of the outhouse where they kept the guinea pig, holding her nose and shaking her head disapprovingly. At that moment she felt no connection with the small, grey-haired, worried woman. The neat lawn and the little flower beds were between them, and Sara sat perched like a bird ready to take off until her small sister Emily came running up the garden and hoisted herself up on the wall. She settled herself beside Sara, pushing back her long fair plaits.

'Why do you sit here all the time?'

'I don't.'

'Yes, you do. I've seen you. Hours and hours and hours. And by the way, I hate your hair. You look like a witch.'

Sara tilted her head round to her sister and screwed up her small pale features. Only the other day she had dyed her hair to match Liam's. She had bought a bottle of rinse-in hair dye, and now her hair was as black as night and Mum said she had ruined herself, her hair had been so pretty, there was no need to pour a great bottle of black all over it. But Sara loved her newly coloured hair because it made her feel a different sort of person. And she *was* a different person! She was out of place in this cooped up garden.

'Well, I like it and if you want to know, my aim is to get away from everybody. It seems like free over there, on the other side of the wall. Ever since Dad died this has been like prison.'

She turned back to the view, one leg crooked, one leg

4

hanging down. She had changed into her jeans - anything to get out of her school uniform, and she unconsciously plucked the neck of her thick, grey jumper, pulling it over her chin and lips then back again.

Emily hesitated for a moment. 'Why are you always grumpy now?'

'I'm not.' Sara let go of her jumper and pursed her lips.

'Yes, you are, and you never used to be like it. You used to draw for me. Remember Pink Rabbit?'

One of Sara's greatest joys had been her drawing. Not that she was that good but she had loved the feeling of the pencil on the page and spent hours doing little else.

'Pink Rabbit!' Sara exclaimed, 'That was ages ago. Everything has changed.' She paused. 'I hate school for one thing. Ruby's my only friend and she's never there. I can't wait to leave. Only four months to go! And then there's Ben. I'm sick of him coming round here after Mum. He's meant to be employing her, not visiting her.'

'I like Ben,' said Emily 'and we do good things at my school. What do you hate about it?'

'Everything. Exams. The way they tell you off all the time.'

'That's because you're no good.'

Sara shrugged her shoulders and Emily sat silently beside her, filling her cheeks with air and slowly expelling it.

'I know something you don't hate.' She turned to her sister with raised eyebrows. 'The white horse.'

It was true that Sara loved the white horse. He was old and stocky and tethered to a tree in a private patch of land that looked over the downs. His nose was always over the fence trying to get food from passers-by and Sara and Emily often fed him with sugar lumps. Emily's small voice broke into her thoughts: 'I know someone else you don't hate. That man who comes to see you. Liam.'

'I hate him most of all.'

Emily pointed to the great unfurling oak tree a little way off. 'Then why did you kiss him under that tree last night?'

When Sara answered spikily - 'You're always spying on me,'

5

her sister went on in a matter-of-fact voice: 'Anybody could see you, especially from my bedroom window. It wasn't even very dark!'

'Well, don't you dare tell anyone!'

Emily ran down the garden and Sara quickly jumped over the wall.

The evenings were beginning to draw out; there was a faint sense of excitement in the mild air. The damp grass discoloured her trainers and wet her ankles as she pushed her way up towards the oak tree. She chewed a piece of grass unthinkingly, then sat down under the budding branches, cross-legged. At this moment a pony galloped by and Sara looked enviously at the rider. It seemed a long time now since she had ridden a horse. When she was twelve she had helped down at the stables with the stable boy from down the road. They mucked out, then took the horses up to the field and back, early in the morning and when it was dark, for a whole year, even when the snow was thick on the ground and her fingers were sticks of ice in her mittens. She could remember as if it was yesterday, the smoke of her breath on the air and the horses' breath clouding their muzzles. She had set her heart on one pony at the stables. He was called Tinker and was not unlike the one who now galloped on the downs. Then one day Tinker had stumbled over a clump of small bushes and broken his leg. They had to shoot him. She often heard that shot in her head. It resounded just as she saw Liam coming over the hill towards her and her heart beat fast. He walked quickly and from a distance looked in good nick, but as he drew near she had to acknowledge his unhealthy pale skin and his black hair wispy round his ears. But his eyes, it was always his eyes that drew her to him, bright as a cat's and liquid green.

He took her in his arms and kissed her. She melted into his body but resisted him at the same time.

'Not here. My sister keeps on spying.'

By now, night weighted the edges of the sky, so that

it seemed to spread flatly down over the land and slowly, imperceptibly move towards them as they hurried on, hand-in-hand. It began to rain and Sara shivered.

'Cold?' Liam put his arms round her again.

Sara stared down at her feet. 'Wet.'

A few yards ahead of them was a small, wooden hut, perhaps at one time used to store the down keeper's tools. Now the tiny square window was broken, the arched roof was almost caving in and the door creaked on its hinges.

'Let's go in there,' said Liam.

Inside was surprisingly dry. There were the remains of old newspapers and piles of hay.

'A tramp's been here,' said Liam, gently pushing Sara down on the hay and kissing her eyes. She fingered the buttons of his denim jacket like a small child and he laughed. 'You're a funny one, Sara.'

They talked easily together as they always had done. Sara found herself telling him about the horse she used to ride.

'How do they shoot horses?' she asked him.

'Don't know, maybe between the eyes,' he said and added to impress her: 'Did you know my brother once tried to shoot me?'

'*Your brother*?' She hardly believed him.

Liam enjoyed telling Sara the story. He was ten at the time. 'Visual aids,' he said, pulling out a photo of himself at about that age that he kept in his wallet. Sara stared for a long time at the little boy squinting in the sunlight, holding hands with his brother Brad, who even at fourteen, she thought, had the blunt features of a bully.

'He always bullied me,' Liam told her. 'Mum and Dad took no notice though I told them what was happening. They never believed it, they couldn't bring themselves to believe it. How could they when half the time they left him to look after me and even paid him. They both had to go to work, see?'

'So what happened?'

'One day when Mum and Dad had gone shopping Brad took Dad's hand gun out of the drawer and led me out into the field at the back of our house. "I could shoot you dead if I wanted to," he told me, brandishing the gun. Just think, Sara, I was only ten at the time and small and thin at that!

"I'll tell Mum," I said but he only laughed. "If you do things will get worse, far worse, not better. Anyway, there's no-one here. There's no-one around at all." Then he put his face right up to mine.

"They've taught me to aim straight if they've done nothing else. I'm one of the best."

"If you shoot me you'll go to prison."

Brad laughed again. "Prison! No-one will ever know. Get up against that fence!"

It was at that moment that John – he was an old man who lived up our street - passed by on the footpath with his black Labrador, Kim. I shouted at him, "Hey! Wait for me." At least I meant to shout but my voice came out thin and weedy just like John's voice. He was a nice man and stopped.

"What's got into you lad? You sound frightened."

I pointed to Brad, "He wants to to - to shoot me."

By now Brad had hidden the gun in his fleece and was smiling inanely.

"That's bunk!" he said. " He's only ten years old and he's already a boot faced liar. I was only trying to cheer him up, that was all."

But I kept walking alongside Kim and John until Brad was out of sight.

John really tried to help me. "You tell your Mum and Dad," he said to me, but I didn't let him know that would be worse than useless. I hung around his house until Mum came home.'

Liam looked hard at Sara. 'Never been so scared in my life. I thought Brad was going to shoot me dead. It was a long time before I discovered it was not a real gun but a replica my father had bought online!'

They both sat up and he tightened his thin pale fingers round her small hands. He looked at her intently.

'There's something else I want to tell you. It's important

you should know. You might even have guessed.'

Rain was trickling down the small, broken window and Sara could hear the horse neighing.

'Come on, tell me,' she said.

Chapter two

Tell me the score

Liam brought out a tin from his frayed jacket pocket and Sara examined it carefully. It was an oblong shape, made from white metal. On the lid was the pattern of a silver dragon flying through bamboo shoots. The dragon's scales were meticulously marked, his eye was fierce and his long jaws were held apart by a silver flame.

'What do you keep in there?'

Liam pursued his own thoughts. 'Take the railway, Gives you the feeling you're part of something. Know what I mean?'

Sara looked puzzled. 'Is that what you wanted to tell me?'

He shrugged his shoulders. 'I was going to be a guard. I'd been a platform assistant for some time and I was going to get trained up. Well, I lost my job.'

'Oh Liam!' All her sympathy went into the words. 'Why did you lose it?'

He put the tin back in his pocket, picked up a piece of the hay, then drew with it. 'Someone shopped me. They got rid of me straight away.'

Sara leaned back and scrutinized him. 'You mean-'

'Didn't think I'd have to spell it out.'

She waited.

'I'm registered. Like Steve.'

Into Sara's mind flashed an image of their first meeting. She had written about it in her diary but she had ended the paragraph with a question mark, because there were things she had not quite understood. That day she had visited Gran, and because Ruby lived in the same road she called on her afterwards. Ruby was just going out to the Boar's Head so Sara went with her. That was where she first met Liam.

'It's the place to be,' said Ruby, in a slightly slurred voice.

'Besides, Dave will be there.'

She had often spoken to Sara about Dave. His mum had had him when she was fifteen, and he'd never known his schoolboy dad. He was a bit all over the place but he was a good-looking boy with a good heart. They were near neighbours and he fell in love with Ruby and she with him. He hadn't made it after school, and now he was into drugs Ruby wasn't so sure about what would happen in the future. 'Who cares?,' she had said to Sara with one of her flashing smiles. 'It's now that counts. It's like us, Sara, Dave and me would do anything for each other.'

Today Ruby was dressed in a thin green see-through top that fluttered over her tight jeans. She wore high-heeled shoes that revealed her painted toes and bangles that dazzled her black arms. She tied a red scarf round her thick curly hair and stood up very straight. To Sara, Ruby always looked glamorous.

Inside the Boar's Head they had all sat round a table. Ruby was next to Dave, and opposite Sara was Steve, a fuzzy-haired boy who talked nonsense in a loud voice. Suddenly he crashed his head down onto the table. Blood oozed down his face and along the oak boards. Liam, who was sitting next to Sara, scraped back his chair nervously, borrowed a tissue from Sara and wiped Steve's face. Then he turned to Sara and said they'd better go. They didn't want to get caught, did they? It was their first encounter and she remembered thinking how thoughtful he was, how good it was to be looked after by a man. Nonetheless she was puzzled by what had happened. She would have to ask Ruby to explain.

The last red flash of the sinking sun speared the window and brought Sara back to the hut.

Liam was speaking in a soft voice. 'Can't get off the dope, that's why I'm registered, like Steve.'

Sara spoke quietly. 'But why?'

Liam shrugged. 'Those bastards out there, they don't know anything. They think they do, they think they can pick you up and cure you but they never do. It's like we're different, see? Like we're not meant to be intelligent or any of that stuff. Like they smile at you and take you in, but all the time they're thinking, he's nothing, he's nothing. He's a black hole and not a star. You know that lyric? Well, you wouldn't because I made it up. No-one's heard of anything I've made up and why should they? *I ain't got no money and no name.*' He was silent for a while. 'Do you remember that rhyme about Mr. Nobody? Well in our house he never took the blame. It was always me.'

He didn't seem to think it was strange to bring in a children's rhyme. His voice was bitter and Sara wasn't sure how to reply. She remembered the first verse, and though it seemed an incongruously childish sort of thing for her to quote, she nonetheless said it to Liam in a mocking sort of way that somehow softened him.

> *I know a funny little man,*
> *As quiet as a mouse,*
> *Who does the mischief that is done,*
> *In everybody's house!*

She fiddled with a button on his jacket and smiled at him. 'Come on, it's not always you. Sometimes old Mr. Nobody is about.' He laughed. 'Take me,' said Sara. 'Mum always blames everything on me, never on my little sister. But that's other people for you. What *they* think doesn't make any difference to us, does it? You're still the same person. So am I.'

'Perhaps we're not,' said Liam. He leaned on one elbow and his eyes were an angry green. 'I'll go on the dole until something else turns up.'

Sara looked round the hut. The smell of damp grass and wind curved through the broken window and made the dry hay and dark wood homely. Liam's confession brought her closer to him. She felt as if she had to protect him.

'Let's make this our meeting place. Always.'

He nodded and drew her towards him. 'I don't know what I'd do without you, Sara. Sometimes things get me down. Without you -'

He held her close as if he never wanted to let her go.

13

They began to make the small, isolated room their own. First Liam brought up a patchwork blanket and two cushions, then he produced a rusty calor gas stove and two cracked blue mugs. No one interfered. Once or twice Mum remonstrated because Sara was always going out, but when she told her she liked to go up onto the downs to read, her mother seemed to accept it.

One day while they were in the hut drinking lager out of the mugs, Liam said, 'Listen, Babe, I feel responsible for you. I'm a lot older than you. There's a lot of difference between eighteen and fifteen.'

Sara snuggled up to him. 'Doesn't feel that different to me.'

He smiled. 'I've been meaning to tell you . This morning I phoned your Mum.'

She pulled away from him angrily. 'I don't know why you have to drag her into it.'

'You know why. If she finds out she might try to put an end to us meeting.'

'It's nothing to do with her.'

Sara mentally pushed Mum away. She belonged to another world. She stood up and looked out of the little window but all she saw were her own thoughts. How dare he phone Mum! How dare he bring her into it! He didn't understand anything. She turned back and watched Liam searching in his pocket, bringing out the dragon tin, rattling it, smiling at her gently as if nothing at all had happened. Maybe she was being silly. She sighed and went back to him. He carefully opened the hinged lid and showed Sara the tiny coloured tablets. 'Es. Different ones.Don't tell no-one. You get seven years for possession.'

He took four and swallowed them down. He leaned towards her and she tried to take one. He shook his head.

'Why not? I'm fed up. What did Mum say?'

'Nothing really. I never said much. I told her I felt responsible for you and wouldn't let anything happen. She didn't seem to know what to say.'

'My Mum never knows what to say,' said Sara, pulling at the tin.

14

'Come on. The other day you promised me I could have some. Come on, Liam.'

'Look, Sara, for the record, I do care for you. Much better if you didn't.' He put the tin back in his pocket but she pulled it out. She stared at the silver dragon, then opened the lid and defiantly took one, two, three pills.

'Gold dust,' he told her and stared back, as if he was partly mesmerised by her action and partly pleased that at last she was moving into his world.

'Oh well, it's up to you. I told you not to. Can't do more.'

They lay down together, facing the little window. The sun had gone. The broken window framed a huge star that slowly moved from right to left. Sara followed it in wonderment until it dawned on her that it was an aeroplane, and behind the aeroplane were the stars that looked small and cold but were really burning up huge gases in unthinkable distances. A dog barked, another answered, a big star slowly and silently crossed the broken window frame.

Liam held her as if she was as delicate as the butterflies he had once caught as a child. He told her they fascinated him, those butterflies, the marking of their wings, the way one wing mimicked the other, their complete metamorphosis from egg to larva to pupa to butterfly. He pinned them down, fragile and bright, onto a velvet cushion in a box. They were his forever, they would never fly away again. He hid the box in the tiny attic of their house and sometimes climbed up there to look at them. He knew they were safe from his brother who could never get through the hole in the ceiling. Then one day Brad poked a broom up through the hole and manoeuvred the box until it tipped out and fell to the floor. There was nothing left but dusty broken bits of wood and a scattering of butterfly wings.

Liam looked down at Sara and strengthened his hold on her.

'This shed's a bit like that attic, dark and private and away from everybody. And you're changing, Sara, though you're not quite a butterfly yet. Just coming out of your chrysalis, just ready to spread your wings.'

She like his poetry words and smiled up at him. He drew

15

back her long black hair and whispered intimately into her ear: 'Let's skip it tomorrow. Let's go somewhere on our own.' He stroked her hair appreciatively. 'All this and a bag of chips, eh?'

Sara's fingers met his, her voice was sibilant. 'Where?'

'Up town,' Liam swayed slightly, 'We'll give ourselves a treat.'

Later that night Sara stood in her night tee shirt with her clothes in a heap at her feet. She stared and stared at her bed, at the uneven hump of bedclothes. When she heard her mother pacing up the stairs she flung herself under the crumpled pile and pulled the blankets over her head.

The door creaked quietly open. She felt her mother sit on the bed. 'Sarey.' It was a long time since she had been called her by this affectionate nickname. Mum's voice was pleading, the anger had gone.

'We must talk.' She gently peeled back the blankets. 'Now listen. I had this phone call. It's important for me to understand. Whoever is this Liam Brake? Where did you meet him?'

Sara shut her eyes tightly. In her mind's eye she could see her mother's worried look, the streaks of grey in her shoulder length hair. She squeezed her eyelids even more tightly so that she would not be tempted to sit up, cuddle her mother and cry.

After a while Mum walked away and from behind the door her voice sounded hurt, clear, angry: 'And another thing . That guinea pig you've neglected for so long. He died this morning.'

Sara waited for the sound of footsteps to fade away, then kicked off the bedclothes. She put on the light and sat bolt upright in her cotton night shirt, hugging her knees and staring straight ahead at the image of herself in the dressing table mirror. She walked over to the glass and looked into her own bright, fragile eyes. What was happening to her? Where was Liam taking her? She picked up her teddy bear, who sat unkempt and in need of sewing in the corner chair, and slipped back into bed with him. Poor Liam! She would write all about this evening in her diary. She got up again and rummaged through her clothes in the chest of drawers until she found the thick exercise book that she kept secretly under her clothes. There were times when she forgot to write in it but mostly she did, especially on the days when there was nothing inside her but loss and emptiness. She went back to bed and watched her hand-writing stream large and uncontrolled from the biro.Was this love, this feeling she would go anywhere with Liam?

Or was it madness?

Was she going mad?

Her body tingled and she felt her jaw muscles tighten. Her heart was beating fast and she felt hot and panicky. I can't stay in, she thought, and carefully opened the bedroom door. It creaked slightly. She waited, shut it behind her, then rushed downstairs. She crept through the living room, opened the small french windows and stepped into the garden. The spring night air blew into her face and a cold, white moon stood above the garden, turning it ghostly.

'I'll spend the night out here.' When the next-door cat sidled up she could have screamed. '*I mustn't. They'll hear.*' She wanted to think about her guinea pig, but her mind was floating somewhere above her, embracing the stars and moon and cat as if they were bright paper cut-outs that were drifting away and away from her. She climbed up the little stone wall. She talked to herself and looked round to make sure no-one was listening. At that moment the moon edged out from a drifting cloud. Its white light struck a cross, stuck in the ground. What was a cross doing stuck at her feet? She knelt down and felt a hump of loose earth. It was the guinea pig's grave. Sara stood up and cried out loud. She ran back towards the house.

The next minute lights from the kitchen were blazing across at her, and her mother was there, in her nightgown, ready to bring her in, hold her, give her a glass of water. Sara drank silently until her mother came over to her and held out her hands. 'Come on, we'll get to bed.'

Upstairs, Sara lay on her back, stretched out under the bedclothes. She stared and stared at the image on the ceiling. There was the guinea pig running about, its nose sniffling, looking at her with bright, blank, innocent eyes. Suddenly it stopped, its eyes blank.

'I wonder what's happening to me,' she thought . She would have given anything to have the innocence, the brightness back. Yet even in the confusion of her mind and body she felt there were things to anticipate, new experiences, a new life perhaps.

Chapter three

Call me up

The next day Sara felt panicky and sick and confused, but she was determined to meet Liam. She rushed out of the house before Mum could catch her and bring her back. She waited under the oak tree, standing in damp grass, looking over the downs. Surely he would come? After all, it was *his* idea. After half an hour she flung down her fleece and lay down on the grass looking up at the huge branches cobbled together above her. It was a fairly mild but windy day and the leaves swayed round them. Maybe he was too ill.

She shut her eyes and remembered when Dad had taken her to St James Park. She was a small child and he had taken her on her own. It was about this time of the year, a fresh, light April day. In the park nothing was still. It seemed as if the busy birds, the wind on the water, the changing pastel colours of the sky were all swirling round her. The ducks splashed forwards to the showers of crumbling bread that she and Dad threw at them. They made her laugh, especially the way they dipped their heads in the water with the bread in their beaks. She remembered how they had a Macdonald's Quarter Pounder each, washed down with diet coke. And on the train back she had sat on Dad's knee because the train was crowded. She felt as if she was sitting on the knee of a king.

Sara began to cry. Liam wasn't like Dad after all. She hung on for an hour, then she wandered home and went back to bed. Dad would never have let her down. Never.

Mum brought her up a drink of hot chocolate. She said nothing as if there was nothing to say. That was Mum all over. She simply didn't know how to put things into words. In the same way Sara couldn't speak to her. She wanted to say, 'Mum, I feel so ill, I feel so sad, I don't know what to do any more,' but she couldn't. She simply drank the hot chocolate and felt sick and anxious. Maybe she should talk to Gran. That was never difficult except that it was sometimes hard to get a word in edgeways.

After school Emily came up to her bedroom and showed her the pink paper rabbit she had made. 'It's for you,' said Emily, 'in memory of the one you once made me. She's a magic rabbit and she'll make you better.'

The rabbit was about a hundred and fifty centimetres high. It was wearing a brown jacket with bright red buttons and brown shorts. A blue ribbon was tied over its ears. It was smiling and holding a twig.

'It's a magic twig,' said Emily. 'It helps you in times of trouble.'

'What's the rabbit called?' asked Sara.

'Twinkle. That's because she's got twinkle toes. Gran says I have twinkle toes too.'

'It's lovely.'

Emily pirouetted round the bed and out of the room.

The next morning Sara woke up with an unexpected feeling of hope. For one thing, she no longer felt ill. Maybe everything would be all right after all. She leaped out of bed and ran to the window. Her bedroom looked out onto the road and she was reassured by the sight of her neighbour's dog, Lily the lab, sniffing at the lamp post and nosing in the grassy verge. When Sara was smaller she had often taken Lily out for a walk. Now there was a shout from the next door house and Lily, who was black and fat, trundled back indoors.

It was a racy day with chinks of sun gleaming behind the flying clouds. Sara thought of Gran and how brave she had been when Dad died. He was her only child, the blessing of her life, she used to say. Yet she didn't go on about it, only tried very hard to comfort Sara and Emily and Mum. She had been house-bound for as long as Sara could remember and one or other of them visited her bungalow nearly every day. She always had little fairy cakes in the larder and put them on a plate beside her fat brown teapot. Gran's neighbour, Aunty Marge, helped her out and she was often there pouring out the tea and passing round the plate. 'Go on, have another one,' Gran would say, 'Make yer hair curl.' Sara smiled as she thought of Gran. She had everything wrong with her but she always made you laugh. She would go and see her – she must remember the key.

That morning she paid extra special attention to cleaning her teeth and brushing her hair. Gran was the only one who said she was 'a beautiful girl.' Mum always found something wrong with her and even Liam never really complimented her on how she looked. She smiled at herself in the mirror. She would go in the early afternoon after Gran had had her rest.

To Sara it was one of the most familiar roads in the village. She had always called for Ruby on her way to school and Gran's house was a little way up the road from Ruby's, at the very top where the fields began. She instinctively stopped outside Ruby's house and scrutinised it for any sign of life. It had looked derelict all the time she had known Ruby. The windows were blank, the white paint on the window frames was burnt off by the sun and the paint on the green front door was peeling off. Maybe Rubes was inside, fast asleep. Sara walked through the gate that swung on one hinge and up the overgrown path. She rang the bell again and again but no-one came. Had Ruby's mother gone off with her lover as she said she would one day? Had Ruby run away with Dave? She knew in her heart something had happened. She rang the bell once again and listened to it echoing through the empty house. Then she turned and hurried up the road.

Unlike Ruby's house there was always a comforting look to Gran's two bedroom bungalow: The window frames were painted white, the wooden door bright blue. The outside walls were pebble dashed and the tiny garden was full of wild bluebells.

Sara let herself in and called out to announce herself. Gran was as usual sitting in the small living-dining room. She looked up at her granddaughter and her wrinkled face broke into a wide smile.

'You look beautiful this morning, Sara.'

Gran was fat and disabled and always wore a tight fitting navy blue pinafore over her jumper and skirt. Her slippers were heeled so she wouldn't slip when she got up from her chair, and beside it she kept a stick with a wide marble holder for her arthritic right hand. Her cheery, small brown eyes always made Sara feel more settled.

'I'll put on the kettle.'

'I wish you'd let me do it,' said Sara.

'Then what would become of me, sitting down all day? Tell you what , you can get out the cakes, Marge bought them for me yesterday and we don't want to give them to the birds.'

Gran slowly shuffled over to the sink, filled the kettle and plugged it in, then took a few paces, turned herself round with her back to the chair, placed her stick beside it and sank down like a heap of cloth.

'That's me lot, you can make the tea.'

Sara brought Gran a mug of tea and put it carefully on the little table beside her chair. Then she put a madeleine cake on a plate and set it beside the tea, just as Gran liked it.

'Bring your own over and pull up that sofa,' said Gran and when Sara was settled she said, 'How are you, are you all right?'

Sara nodded.

'That's not quite what yer Mum tells me. You know me, I have to get things off me chest. I'll have my say, then it's finished.' She took a sip of tea and a bite of cake, then stroked her navy blue pinafore with her white, freckled, wrinkled hands.

'It's hard for you lot today. God out of the window and everything haywire! But it won't do, Sara. It's no good joining the bandwagon because your Dad's died. Anger won't get you nowhere.'

'I'm not angry,' said Sara, half hiding behind her mug. 'Not this morning. Not this morning, Gran.' But Gran went on looking at her and finally Sara said in a low voice: 'I just don't believe in anything any more, that's all.'

'It's your age,' said Gran, ' and the world we live in.'

Sara flung her head back and drank the tea. It was a relief to listen to her grandmother like this. It made her feel even more deeply the possibility of becoming her old self again. She remembered those visits years ago when all she thought about was how many fairy cakes she would be allowed to eat. I never think of things like that now, she thought.

They sat comfortably together, drinking and eating until Gran had finished and Sara had cleared away.

"Now listen to me,' said Gran. 'there's no need to act funny just because you don't believe in anything any more. Whatever would your Dad think? He'd like you to work hard, I know. So if you care what he would think, and I know you do, you must put your head down and do your homework hard and never turn a blind eye to all the dangers you might meet. You'll get caught that way. You're a beautiful girl and I have every faith in you.'

'Mum hates my hair.'

Gran looked quizzically at Sara. 'Well, it's a bit dark but quite glamorous. I don't know why people make such a fuss about hair. When I was young my hair came right down to my waist.'

Sara laughed. 'I bet you didn't dye it black.'

'I never went that far,' said Gran, 'but then I didn't have a boyfriend like you at your age. '

'Mum doesn't like my boyfriend.'

'She's worried,' said Gran. 'You have to be careful, you know. There. That's my say.'

She reached for the remote control on the little table then put on the television spectacles she had bought from a mail order. The advertisement had promise her 'wonderful sight' and since she had no faith in opticians and her eyes were dimming with cataracts, she wrote off for them. They were made in shiny red plastic, and looked like a telescope on the nose. Sara had to laugh.

'Get away with you,' said Gran, 'the funny thing is I can hear better when I got them on. I can hear everything as clear as a bell.'

Sara kissed Gran goodbye and thanked her. She always felt better after she'd seen Gran.

Sara's sense of well being stayed with her all the way home and when Emily asked her to go with her to collect the eggs from Ben, she went without protest.

It was late afternoon and they walked over the downs to Ben's unkempt farmhouse. Shadows of clouds were racing across the hills between blue patches of sky. Every so often rain spurted down.

When Ben answered the door, Sara watched Emily blink through her blond, overgrown fringe.

'A dozen eggs, please, Ben.' Emily carefully put the basket down on the stone step that was worn by generations who had scraped and knocked their muddy boots against it.

'She wants to please him,' thought Sara.

She looked round. The distant fields had been sold off a long time before Ben came here, and now there were only two fields left. She knew from Mother that Ben ran the place part-time as a smallholding and spent another two days a week helping his friend in his small sweet shop in Clapham. He didn't really like this life. He wanted to join his son in Australia and live on a ranch. He was determined to do that one day.

Sara watched the chickens running in circles in front of the house, pecking idiotically at the ground.

'We'll have to hunt for the eggs,' said Ben. He stepped back into the dark hall and took a hat and raincoat off the hall stand. He was a middle-aged man with a mild manner and a soft voice. His face was weather-beaten and lined and his hair was grey. Much too old for Mum, thought Sara, why doesn't she stick to cleaning for him, she's good at that. As they opened the front door a slab of light fell on the polished brown tiles. They went out together into the muddy forecourt, where grass grew up among half-sunken bricks.

'I like hunting for eggs,' said Emily, pushing back her fair plaits and looking up at Ben who laughed indulgently at her, then turned to Sara with an encouraging smile. Mum had told her all about Ben. She had met him in the days when she went to church, just after Dad died. He had no children and his wife had died ten years ago. His help had just left him to have a baby so Mum told him she needed to make a bit of money and unlike most people she loved cleaning. Months later Mum had told Sara: 'He's lonely, it's a shame for a good man to be lonely.'

What did she mean by that? Was Mum trying to tell her something? No-one in Sara's heart could ever replace Dad. From that moment she was angry with Mum and wary of Ben.

But today things looked a little different. She found, despite herself, that she was relaxing. He was a calm man, you had to give him that.

They found the eggs in all sorts of odd, muddy, straw-laden places and at each find Emily squeaked with delight and carefully put the egg into the basket.

'They're much dirtier than shop ones. I shouldn't think it's very easy to clean them.'

Ben lifted up one of the eggs, golden brown and criss-crossed with pieces of brown and yellow straw.

'A bit of farmyard dirt doesn't hurt anyone,' he said.

Afterwards they had glasses of orange juice in the kitchen and slices of sponge cake that Mum had obviously made. The stone slab floor was scrubbed clean and the red and green gingham curtains framed the old sparkling windows. It looked as if it was already Mum's house. Sara sighed and watched Emily count out the money from her purse, while Ben put the eggs into two cardboard containers and gave them to her to put in the basket.

'I tell you what,' said Ben, once they were outside, 'I have a moment to spare. I'll carry the eggs over the downs for you. I've something to ask your mother.'

By now the rain had stopped and the sky was awash with shades of grey and damp blue. Sara marched silently beside Ben who suddenly said, 'Listen! So many birds singing after the rain.' He stopped and lifted his red, weather-worn face to the sky and with both hands shielded his creased blue eyes.

'A skylark, that's rare nowadays.' He turned to Sara. 'There used to be a lot on the downs.'

Sara didn't answer. They were at the top of a slope and she could see the hut, huddled into the grass. There was a tiny, indistinct figure beside it. Was it Liam, waiting for her? She felt torn between two worlds. They reached home and on the doorstep Ben handed over the eggs, and told Mum awkwardly about a Charity Ball up in London. It was all night, it would mean staying overnight at the hotel - but even the hotel was

25

donating something to the Childrens' Society. Saturday week. Surely she was free!

He fidgeted awkwardly. He's a brown, wrinkled outdoor man, thought Sara. It's only because he wants Mum that he's going to this stupid dance.

'What a lovely idea.' Mum looked down at Emily. 'You could go to Mia's, and -' she faced Sara anxiously. 'What about going round to Gran's? I won't be able to visit her that weekend and I know she loves to see you.'

Sara nodded in an offhand way. She had a photograph of her mother and father dancing at the Works Night Out. Had Mum no memories, no loyalty? Well, *she* had loyalty, if her mother didn't. She walked quickly out of the room and ran upstairs. She no longer felt as if everything would come out right. How could it, when Mum had forgotten Dad?

Chapter four

Palm to palm

That evening she met Liam in the hut.

'I don't see why not,' she said to Liam when he slowly opened his dragon tin. 'Other people do what they like.'

After that he waited for her every evening and that week she never failed him. The hut was like a sanctuary from all that made her life difficult and she grew to enjoy its secrecy and its peril. She wasn't dumb, she knew what she was doing and it wasn't that she couldn't help it. No, it was a gesture, her secret, angry response to all the things she found difficult. Liam caressed her gently, seducing her with his pills.

'Angel dust,' he said, opening the dragon tin. 'That will put you somewhere else.' He laughed, but that evening Sara was cautious. She knew Ruby had a friend who nearly died because she'd snorted too much PCP*. She had ended up in a coma and somehow or other had never been quite the same again. Through the window she could hear the old white horse neighing not far away, and it took her back to those cold icy mornings when she went down to the riding school and mucked out the stables. She knew she had to keep hold of that memory if she was ever to find herself again. It was like the magic thread Ariadne gave Theseus to fight the Minotaur in the labyrinth. She remembered how Dad used to read to her at night from a book of Greek myths. This sort of time. Here! Now! What would Dad say, what would Dad do? But if Dad was alive everything would be different!

She could hear his voice, deep and expressive, and feel his breath on her cheek as he read to her. 'Before Daedalus had left Crete, he had given Ariadne a magic ball of thread, and instructed her how to enter and leave the labyrinth that led to the Minotaur – that great raging monster who killed nine Athenian maidens and youths every nine years.'

'Do you know about the Minotaur?' she asked Liam who was lying beside her on the ragged rug with his eyes shut. He moved vaguely.

'Used to,' he said, 'Don't remember things as well as I used to.'

She leaned up on one elbow. 'Who gave you the angel dust?'

He laughed. 'Si. It's not difficult to get – it's getting money for it that's hard.' He went silent for several minutes and then murmured. 'It's a long story. Would you like to know how I met Si?'

'Tell me.'

He'd known Si forever- well it seemed like forever. They'd been school mates and sometimes his friend protected him from his brother's bullying. Si was adventurous but somehow soft. 'A bit like me, I suppose,' said Liam. Si played about at school but when he left he wanted to go round the world, he wanted to earn money. He bumped into someone who told him how to do that without trying very hard. So Si started to deal drugs and one day, when they were out in the field at the back of Liam's house, he said to Liam: 'Look, I know that brother of yours never stops getting at you. I've got a way out, if you're interested. It costs a bit of course, but you have pocket money, don't you, and your mum will give you anything you want, won't she?'

'That's how it all started,' said Liam, 'me and him in that field, both smoking pot and feeling we could kill any monster, even the Minotaur.'

Through the haze of those evenings Sara thought she could put together the jigsaw of events and people who made Liam what he was. She almost left him out of the equation, as if his willpower had flickered out a long time ago with the beatings his brother gave him. She wrote down Liam's story in her diary and made notes on his family.

Liam's Mum: kind protective hard working. Worked in a sweet shop to earn extra money that went on Liam. Always willing to give in to her son. Didn't do much for Brad which might have driven him to bully Liam.

Liam's Dad: Hard working office manager. Not much time for his family. Is he having an affair with his secretary? Once Liam found his Mum crying out 'I don't believe it, I don't believe a word. How dare that Hannah phone me up like that. How dare she!'

Tonight Liam told me proudly it was from that moment that his mum took up with him, almost like a substitute for her husband, giving him everything he wanted, listening to him but never hearing anything she didn't want to hear. A dumb kind confused woman. I still don't know what she looks like.

Si: a great friend to Liam who does his best to help him get through like Liam is helping me now. Or am I confused like his mum?

Brad: He's in Afghanistan, a war hero. Nowadays no-one will ever believe what he did to his brother. Now he is praised for killing and his Dad does nothing but speak of him proudly. He's made good, he's a strong, dedicated soldier – how can he compare his two sons? He despises Liam more and more.

Liam needs me and I need him.

Sara remembered how once they went for a walk and Liam spoke of how his father hated him. His mother was different: she was one of the best.

It was Friday and Sara had gone upstairs after supper. She flung open the window and leaned out to find Emily in the garden racing the shadow of clouds that slipped easily up the sloping grass.

'I wish I was like that,' she thought. As she looked at Emily she became sharply aware of how she was changing. She had no measuring tools to hand, only moments like this and one or two things Mum and Gran had said and that she tried to dismiss.

'I won't see Liam this evening,' she thought. 'I'll go and see Gran. I'll tell her I'll stay with her.' She was proud of her resolve but as she passed Ruby's house, she was stopped by a shout from the upstairs window. To her surprise there was Ruby waving, smiling, telling her to wait. A minute later the front door opened and in a rush of affection they hugged each other as if they hadn't been together for years. *Someone who understands*, thought Sara, *someone who really understands.*

Ruby began to sing their song in her rich voice:

'It's a lonely journey on the road,
no stopping with this load,
feet are aching and your body's sore
there's no running any more.
And your heart says it's enough,
winter time and the living's rough,
when your bed's just a wooden floor
there's no running any more.'

Sara looked at her with admiration. 'Rubes, that sounds great.'

Ruby examined Sara. 'And you look cool today. Black hair suits you, it really does. Makes you look more grown-up.'

Sara smiled. 'I love your gear.'

Ruby was wearing sleek black jeans and a blue frilly top that matched the blue of her heavy earrings. Her sandals were gold and her painted toenails gleamed between the straps.

Where've you been, Ruby? I haven't half missed you.'

'We've had a brill time at the squat. Went to the Squatters Estate agent – you know, the one in Shoreditch. Well, they come up with something really good. It's a derelict council property. It's huge like a mansion.'

'Ruby, you are funny. You sound like my mum. She's house proud.'

Ruby's eyes glittered. 'That's not the right word for it. More pleased to have somewhere to go with other people in the house. There's lots of rooms for all of us. You've got to come up, you really have. Liam would like it I know. It's not far from where Si hangs out. A squat costs nothing. You can't be turned out unless they have an eviction order, and I don't think anyone knows we're there. You ought to come with Liam. By the way, how are you feeling about Liam?'

Sara smiled. 'We're really close but I don't think he understands like you do. He's out of it most of the time.'

'Sounds like me. Well, there's no-one to stop me, is there?'

'Then what are you doing here?'

'We've come back to collect a few things.'

The street lamp by the gate went on and Sara stared at Ruby's large brown glistening eyes. She felt confused by the world her friend was describing. Why live up there when you had a house near the downs? Why was it so much better?

'Freedom,' said Ruby as if she had read Sara's thoughts. 'Mind you, at the moment my mum's not here and there's a nasty letter from the landlord. If Mum doesn't pay up – and she won't – we'll be out in the street.'

'That's terrible, Rubes. You should tell them at school. They might be able to do something.'

'School. No thanks! I'm not going back to school. I was sixteen last week, and I won't get my exams- well, maybe music, but what's the point? I told them so and they had to accept it. I really can't go back for help now.'

'Rubes, this is serious. Where *is* your Mum?'

Ruby's voice sounded ironic. 'She says she's with her sister who was taken ill. She says she's looking after her. She says I've got to get a job. The truth is she doesn't care about me. Anyhow,' Ruby raised her thick shaped eyebrows, 'I don't believe this business of her sister. I think she's off with that squeeze of hers.'

Sara nodded with understanding: 'My Mum's going out tomorrow night with this man she cleans for. I hate him.'

Ruby spoke with genuine surprise: 'I thought your Mum never went out.'

'She doesn't. This is so-called special. He's called Ben and he's far too old for her. He's taking her out to some charity ball. Emily's staying the night with her friend Mia.'

'What about you?'

'I might stay with my Gran.'

They started to move up the road. Suddenly Ruby stopped by another lamp post. 'How about a party?'

Sara looked at her blankly, 'I don't like parties.'

Ruby tried again: 'We could have some fun in your empty house.'

'What about yours?'

' Let's throw a coin for yours or mine.'

She jingled some change in the back pocket of her jeans and brought out a ten p piece.

'I don't want a party,' said Sara, but this time she sounded hesitant and Ruby smiled at her. 'You'll see, it's fun. There won't be another chance. Heads or tails? Whoever wins holds the party.'

'Tails,' said Sara. Ruby's rich presence suffused her, there was always a warmth in the air when her friend was around. Ruby tossed the coin in the air and it fell lightly onto the gravel path. They both bent over it. 'Tails,' said Ruby,' We'll come to yours.'

They dawdled on to the next lamp post. It shone mistily down and Sara plucked at a garden hedge and threw a handful of budding leaves into the air. For a second they glinted in the lamp light like little pieces of glass - then they fell and were lost onto the pavement. Ruby began to sing the song she had made up about a year ago when her Mum had walked out yet again. It had become their song, a sign of their friendship. They sang the chorus together.

> 'But I'll be running through the wind and rain,
> going there and back again.
> Don't go asking where I'll roam,
> 'cos I've got no home.
> 'cos I've got no home.'

Sara smiled as they held the palms of their hands together. 'I'll never dump you Rubes, never.'

'Friends forever.'

After a while Ruby began to speak as if everything about the party had already been decided. 'At your place tomorrow night, then. I'll get it sorted.'

'Say my Mum finds out?'

They stood and looked at each other at the next lamp post.

'Come on. Why should she?'

There seemed no point going up to Gran's house now so they walked back together. *Serve Mum right for going out with Ben.* Ruby looked at Sara with her rich, warm gaze. 'Freedom, chick, freedom.

Ruby was right. She had to break out else, else…she would never get over her grief. Gran would be all right without her. After all she was mostly on her own, sitting there with those daft glasses watching the football and the gardening programmes as if she was preparing herself for another sort of life. She wouldn't be hurting Gran.

Sara turned to Ruby and they hugged each other. Ruby was the only person in the world who gave her unconditional warmth , the sense of real togetherness. She'd once read a book about soul friends. That's what Ruby was, her soul friend, her anam cara.

'I'll go and tell Liam,' she said.

Ruby smiled that wide, warm smile. 'He'll be waiting for you, that's for sure.'

But when Sara reached the hut it was empty.

Chapter five

No stopping

Saturday night, nine o'clock. They were banging and shouting their way into the house, laughing and screaming, dumping down bottles and cans on the carpet, girls in brightly coloured flimsy tops - orange, red, green, yellow, black - over torn jeans or short skirts. Carnival faces passed Sara, smiling, joking, smoking, kids she had never met, trampling through the rooms Mum so carefully cleaned, taking glasses and mugs from cupboards and shelves, putting on lights, putting off lights, mocking and playing their own cd's, talking into their mobiles. Who were they? How did they get here?

Someone bumped into her. He was large and ungainly and he smiled as if he was doing it to get his own way.

'Don't know who you are.'

'Doug's friend. They call me Big Curt. See my muscles,' he joked, holding up his arm and feeling its firmness with a large hand. 'Boxing,' he said, 'that's what does it.' He took one look at Sara's confused and childish expression and quickly left her, pushing his way through the smoke and noise.

Sara turned to a girl she'd seen in the pub, 'Do you know who Doug is?'

'Kit's friend – you know, the one who knows Rick.'

'Rick who knows Liam?'

'That's it. That's how I'm here.'

'Liam's not come.'

'Not in a fit state.'

Last night when Sara had left the empty shed, her feeling of excitement had oozed away like the air in one of those balloons Dad had once blown up, then by mistake shrivelled with a kick of his boot. She had the same feeling now. She understood it was Ruby's excitement she had felt, not her own. Ruby who admitted she'd been folded for days as if that was the way she was searching for freedom.

She shouted to someone passing whom she vaguely recognised. 'Where's Ruby?'

Someone answered: 'Changed her mind - she's gone up the squat with Dave.'

'But it was because - '

'Things happen.'

Sara felt a gush of panic. Without Ruby, without Liam, what was the point of all this? A loud tinkling noise interrupted her thoughts.

'Oh God, they've smashed a vase. They're trampling on the bluebells.' She fumbled in the pocket of her jeans. She had taken some Angel Dust pills from the dragon tin and now she stuffed them down her throat. This way she wouldn't care too much about what was happening.

Someone turned out the lights and turned up the volume of the music. A voice sung over the crowded rooms as if her life depended on it. People drew together into couples, danced closely, sat closely, lay down closely.

Sara shoved her way through the house. There were dim figures in the hall, up the stairs, on the landing, everywhere. She pushed open her bedroom door and breathed a sigh of relief. No-one was there. She stretched out, waiting for Liam. Surely he would come? The door opened and she looked up eagerly. But it wasn't Liam, it was Big Curt who came in with a swagger. He launched himself on the bed, held her down and placed his full lips on hers. She struggled and screamed, her voice filled with a sudden, sharp anguish. She tried to push him away. 'Get off! Get off!' she shouted but he was strong, and determined and held her down in a harsh grip. She twisted her head towards his arms and bit his wrist.

'You bitch!' he whispered menacingly and squeezed her breathless. At that moment the door swung open and a voice cried, 'You all right in here?'

'No!' whispered Sara. Curt cursed and rolled off her and Sara sat up crying.

Curt's voice was low and gruff. 'Who do you think you are?'

He put up his fists and Sara heard a familiar voice saying, 'If you fight I'll call the police.'

It was the stable boy from the past. He was a man now, stocky, brown haired and with the same warm brown eyes. In her panic she couldn't remember his name. Oh yes, Paul.

'You must be joking,' said Curt, 'The Fuzz don't come to parties. You don't know nothing! Get out of my way.'

He pushed Paul to one side, looked at Sara in disgust, then shrugged his shoulders and went out, muttering as he went through the door.

Sara didn't move. Tears rolled down her cheeks and Paul wiped them away with a tissue. She caught her breath, her eyes glittered as she smiled. Paul had always been good to her but all she felt was disappointment. *Liam, where are you? Why haven't you come? Where are you? What are you doing?*

Paul felt in his pocket. 'Here's a tissue for you to keep. Have to give you something, after all these years.' She was touched, it seemed a long time since she had been treated with such calmness and kindness. She crumpled up on the bed. After a while she looked up. 'Paul, why are you here?'

'The Olds. They can't stand the noise. They thought I could do something. I had no idea it was as bad as this!'

Sara wiped her tears with the back of her hand and went over to the mirror. 'Real glamour girl I am!' Mascara smirched her blotchy cheeks and she wiped it off with tissue, powdered her face, brushed her dishevelled hair, then went downstairs with Paul, weaving her way behind him through oblivious couples. Paul was someone from her other life, before Dad died, before they moved, before she saw no point to anything. Surely he could make them all go away? He turned round and took her hand.

'Where have you been hiding for two years,' he said. 'This scene -' He looked round, 'It isn't yours, Sara, I know it isn't. You've never liked parties.'

She was comforted by his dark, stocky presence.

'Can't you get them out, Paul? My Mum'll do her nut. She

mustn't know anything about this.'

Paul put on his big cowboy stance. 'Leave it to me, kid.'

But it wasn't as simple as that, and it was in the early hours of the morning that the last person left. Afterwards they cleaned the house, hid the bottles and cans, swept the floor, aired the rooms.

At four o'clock in the morning Paul went out into the garden and picked some damp end-of-season bluebells and brought them in.

'Half of them are dead,' said Sara.

'Couldn't see what I was doing,' said Paul. 'Let's bung them in another vase. Your mum might not notice.'

Sara yawned, too tired to do anything else. 'Do you think everything looks all right?'

'No one would know.'

'Thanks Paul.'

'Hey,' he handed her a piece of paper, 'Take my mobile number just in case.'

'Thanks.' She stuffed it in her pocket, said good-bye and climbed the stairs. She felt grateful but muddled. Paul was from her childhood and was stuck there even though she had just seen him. If only it was Liam who had come to the rescue.

She was afraid to be on her own. She put Paul's mobile number into her contacts just in case she had to call him. Say Curt was hiding in a cupboard waiting for her? She lay on the bed with her eyes wide, listening for every creak, every sound, but after a while she was too tired to keep a vigil and fell asleep.

It was the afternoon when Mum shook her awake. 'Sara, look at me. What have you been up to?' There was an edge of panic in Mum's voice. 'What happened last night? There's a funny smell everywhere, burns in the carpet, broken glass in the bin, cups chipped. The house looks as if it's been invaded.'

She had gone to the top of the garden. At first she only saw a brown pony swerving down the path. Then she caught sight of bottles and cans lying about on the other side of the wall. When she looked back on the garden side of the wall, she found more bottles near the guinea pig's grave and another pile glinting on the compost heap.

'How could you?' Mum walked over to the window. 'There were other things back in the house. Funny cigarette butts in the dustbin, my best vase broken up, the larder raided.' She turned round and held up something in her fingers. 'An army button. Where did the army button come from?'

Sara didn't answer, she huddled under the bed clothes and blocked her ears. Mum shouted: 'You had a party here, didn't you? How could you? It was my one night away, my one night of enjoyment. How could you do it?'

Sara flung off the bedclothes and looked defiantly at her mother. 'It wasn't my fault. I didn't mean it to happen. I met Ruby, that's all. It was her idea. *I* didn't think of it.'

'But *you* let it happen.' Now they were shouting at each other.

'I couldn't help it. I didn't mean it to happen. When they were all here I couldn't stop them. I hated them all! I hated them all!' She put her head down on the pillow and sobbed.

Mum pulled her up angrily and faced her. 'Whatever you say, there's no excuse. You needn't have let it happen. I'm sick and tired of you.' She slapped Sara's tear-stained face. It was the first time in many years that she had slapped her.

'You're keeping bad company, Sara, and I'm not having it.'

'He wasn't even here,' shouted Sara, staring defiantly into Mum's bewildered, hurt grey eyes.

Mum paced the room and then turned back to Sara.

'I'm putting an end to all this. You're not like my daughter any more. You're like someone else, another person, a stranger in the house.'

'I am a stranger in the house,' shouted Sara, as her mother walked out.

Sara stared out of the window. Somewhere in the back of her mind she knew that when she had accepted the everyday routine, her exterior life at any rate, had run very smoothly: like being nine, then ten, then eleven. It was all right then. 'Now I can't stop things happening,' she thought, 'They just happen.'

39

For a long time she listened to Emily chanting a skipping song at the end of the garden.

'I'll say sorry to Mum.'

She went down to the bright kitchen that was smelling of warm toast and honey. She stood awkwardly by the door and said woodenly, 'I'm sorry.'

Her mother looked up. She went over to Sara and put her hands on her shoulders. 'We want you back with us like it used to be.'

But in the evening, when the time to meet Liam came, Sara found herself slipping through the back door while the others were watching the television, compelled, in a way she did not understand, to do something utterly secret, utterly silent. Of course Mum was right. After all, she didn't want to be a stranger any more. But first she had to sort things out with Liam, in her own way, privately

'Been a funny sort of day,' said Liam, stretching out on the patchwork blanket. 'Come on. Snuggle down. It's not very warm.'

The words disarmed Sara. They suggested security, but at the same time they filled her with excitement. When she was with Liam she felt a baby and a woman at the same time.

But she was still upset, 'Why didn't you come to the party? It was for you. I wanted you there, Liam. I wanted you and none of the others. Why didn't you come?'

Liam looked back at her with bright yet opaque eyes. Sara knew he was living an intense, secret world, now perhaps, the only place he knew.

'Stoned out of my mind. That's why I didn't come. I don't know how it happened really. Well, I suppose I do. I went back to find my mum but she wasn't there. My dad was. I thought maybe just this time he'd bail me out, give me something to get on with. You know, just for once. But he didn't. Instead he talked to me all the time as if I was a nobody,' He put on an angry voice. '*Who wants a son like you, you must be a throwback, they say there's always a skeleton in the cupboard. Well, you're the bloody skeleton in ours and the sooner you get out the better.*' Then Mum came in and they had a row, and when my Dad stalked down to the shed, she gave me what I needed. Well, she always does, she's kind, you see, she understands. Well, I overdid it. You can't blame me, can you, not when my Dad tells me I'm a scraping off the floor. I tell you, Sara, I can't take much more of it.'

Sara pushed herself up on one elbow and looked at him.

'There are other ways of doing this. You don't have to go down that path.'

He shrugged his shoulders. 'Sara, you forget, it's the path I've followed for a long time.' He looked at his pale fingers with their long nails. 'It's being out of work, I suppose. Not using my hands, not using anything, it seems like there's a screen between me and the whole world. All except us lot. We're friends, we're good friends, all of us. Like we muck in together, help each other out, score together. But out there,' he nodded at the window that was dotted with stars, 'Nothing seems to go right. It's like I wasn't meant to live in that world.' They were silent and then he took Sara's hand. 'I can see from the look in your eyes that I disappoint you. I can't help it, Sara, and you're the only one who really helps me.' He held her tightly. 'I'm sorry I let you down, I really am.'

Sara was touched. She sat up and hugged her knees. 'Liam, I've been thinking we should both try to start again. Everything's been so awful. Don't laugh at me, Liam, the day I went out with Emily I felt almost happy and normal. That's how I want it to be for us.'

He didn't answer. He pulled her down towards him and kissed her and with all the power of his age and sex suppressed her little desire for innocence. He loved her, he was going to make things better for her. She knew that if she loved him back she must lose her old self. There was no other way.

The week before Easter heralded the snow. Daffodils that had come early, cherry blossom, budding lilac, tight-fisted chestnuts, all were caught and frozen in the snowstorms. It was not only the weather that had taken a turn for the worse. For several nights in a row, Sara came home late, bright-eyed, defiant, untouchable. Her mother was angry, and one part of Sara understood why her mother's exhaustion and loneliness toppled over into a torrent of abuse.

'You must stop all this. Look at your room - orange peel everywhere, cups of mouldy tea, pieces of paper screwed up, it's like Bedlam. And what about that diary? Yes, I have read it, Sara.'

Sara was silent and her mother left her alone..

Later, while Emily was playing with a friend, they found themselves in the living room together. Mum switched off the television and stood in front of Sara with the diary open. In a deliberately harsh voice she read one page out loud. She glared at Sara, closed the book and began to cry. When she had recovered she opened the book again. 'Look at it. Look at it!'

In places the writing was large and uncontrolled and dotted with strange words, Liam's words. The entries were bold and bare; Liam had given her daughter crack, LSD, ecstasy - given them...given them?

'And you never refused?'

Sara tightened her lips.

'That's not all. What's all this about lovemaking, truancy, illness, fear of The Fuzz' –

Mum closed the diary and her grey eyes searched her daughter. 'I've come to the end, Sara. I can't stand it any more. Liam is evil, he has a hold on you, he could easily make you pregnant. There's only one thing I can do now.'

Sara looked at Mum: *I want you to rescue me. I hate you, leave me alone. I love you, I'm sorry.* Then she felt as if she didn't care at all. It had got beyond everything.

'I don't care what happens any more,' she said and walked out of the room. She wandered into the garden, then over the wall. The hut seemed the only place where she could live without being told off. She sat on the patchwork blanket, waiting for Liam, trying to think. Her mind was full of memories chasing each other: the times Liam had equipped the hut, even brought up air cushions. 'Found them in the attic,' he had said, laughing. 'We're making a real home of it. Far from the madding crowd.'

They were doing that book at school. Had he read it? Yes, he wasn't ignorant. And tonight they would celebrate. He had another job, on the buildings.

Sara sighed. Nothing seemed to come of that job. Everything he did fell flat. She was wondering why as he came in.

'You look done-in.'

'Mum found my diary.'

Liam paced the shed. 'You shouldn't keep a diary, darling. Now she knows everything.'

Sara nodded. She thought he might be angry, but instead he pushed her down onto the patchwork quilt. 'No point worrying,' he said, opening his dragon tin. 'Smack. Let's have a smoke.'

They had begun to smoke heroin now, especially if something had happened. 'Nothing like this anywhere,' she thought. 'Just us, floating.' She cupped her chin with her hands and stared at the stars in the window. Liam was right. Out there they were not breathing the same air as she was; it was an alien world. Here in the hut her experience with Liam was intensely, defiantly private.

Chapter six

Count the cost

After school on Monday, Sara came home to a strangely silent house. Where was Emily? It seemed important to hear her skip and sing. She half wondered if Emily was in bed with her toys and went upstairs to look round. The silence was strange and as she ran down the stairs an ominous feeling came over her. What had happened? Her mother was in the kitchen bending rather intently over the kettle.

'Where's Emily?'

Mum looked up and spoke casually. 'She's round at Mia's. I thought we'd have a quiet tea together.'

She sensed something odd in her mother's manner, something tentative and uneasy. They ate and watched the television. Afterwards Sara kept to her room, did her hair, toyed with her homework. When the doorbell rang she jumped up. She opened the door and heard a deep voice.

'Please don't be alarmed. We have got to talk with your daughter. Is she in?'

Sara strained to hear Mum's reply. She rushed back into her bedroom. It was too late to get away. Her mother knocked on the door and came in.

'I'm busy, what do you want?'

'There's someone to see you.'

'Who is it?'

'Come down, please.'

'I'm tidying my things.'

Mum spoke with a trace of anxiety and anger, 'Come down, Sara.'

'You haven't told me who it is.'

At last she clumped down the stairs and into the kitchen. There was a man and a woman there drinking tea. Half a dozen explanations crossed her mind. Maybe Mum had met them at

45

the dance. Maybe they were Ben's friends. Maybe they were Mia's parents. She anxiously fiddled with her hair. There was a funny atmosphere in the room as if they were all waiting for her. She tried to run back up the stairs but her mother stopped her, and the man, in a brown reefer jacket, stepped forward.

'Detective Sergeant Freeman, and this is Police Constable Ryan.' He pointed to the young woman who was with him. She was dressed in a smart brown suit. They could have been anyone. Why didn't they wear their police uniform? Sara looked at Mum who was showing no surprise. How could Mum do this to her? How could she bring herself to allow The Fuzz to come in? She was filled with hatred and looked round for an escape route. There was nowhere to run. Three falsely smiling faces were blocking the whole room.

'This is an informal visit, Sara, don't be frightened. Come and sit down.'

There was nothing for it so reluctantly Sara dragged a chair away from the kitchen table and sat down silently. She felt like a mouse in a cage.

The others were close to the table, their elbows leaning on it, their hands full of notepaper and biros. Sara refused to draw up her chair so Detective Sergeant Freeman leaned forward towards her.

'We have reason to believe, Sara, that your friend Liam Brake has been supplying you with drugs. It would help us enormously if you could give us a straight answer.'

Sara was ready for the question. Liam had told her all about The Fuzz and had drilled her several times. 'Don't be driven into corners, don't play ball, just look as if you're playing ball.' A look of defiance settled on her face.

'That's not true.'

'I thought you were a sensible girl, even if that boyfriend of yours isn't. At fifteen you should know better.'

Sara fingered her long, black hair and fixed her gaze on the wall behind Detective Sergeant Freeman. There was a picture of a National Trust garden they had once visited with Dad. The lawn was so green it looked as if it had been washed by rain. In the middle was a fountain and a bird dipping its beak into the water.

'We need to know,' said Detective Sergeant Freeman with what looked like a smile. 'You won't come to any harm, I promise you that.'

But Sara went on staring at the picture as if that garden was her only escape. Then the Detective Sergeant gave up his kind approach and spoke in a sharper voice of things he had seen, incidents where they had been watched. The policewoman fiddled amiably with the handle of her bag and Detective Sergeant Freeman's voice became louder.

Tears streamed down Sara's cheeks.

'I think we should all have a cup of tea,' said Mum quickly. She gave Sara some hot sweet tea and Sara stared into the brown depths of the cup to try and stem the tide of confusion that was overcoming her defiance. There was a kiss in the middle of the tea and she fixed her eyes on it so that she could assemble her thoughts. It was no good, she was too frightened, she couldn't think at all, she could only feel the thump, thump of her heart as she swirled the kiss round and round with a teaspoon.

Detective Sergeant Freeman began to talk more quietly and Sara looked up briefly. His elbow rested on the table, his brown hair shone under the lamp that Mum had put on to cheer up the room, although it was not yet dark. His brown eyes softened and in a level tone he explained to Sara the terrible danger she was in.

'One thing leads to another. How do you think Liam got into this state? You do understand he is in a bad state?'

Sara shrugged her shoulders.

'It must have struck you that he wasn't always a registered drug addict. He was just like you at the beginning.' He kept his voice even, leading her on, little by little, talking in a fatherly way. It was that fatherly voice that made Sara break her silence. Her cheeks flushed as she spoke.

'He only gave me stuff because I asked for it,' she said, 'It was all my fault, I wanted to try out the Magic Dust. You see, I liked the name and it was so easy. They were little tablets mixed with mint. Well, the next thing was he gave me heroin. He called it "The Experience everyone should have." '

Detective Sergeant Freeman nodded to his companion and

Sara held her breath. She had seen that intimate nod before from Miss Archer as if it said, *I told you so.* Had she said something disastrous? The thought enveloped her like a tightening net: *I should have kept quiet, Liam always said shut up in front of The Fuzz.*

She asked: 'What are you going to do to Liam?'

'Talk to him, as we talk to you.'

'That's right,' said Mum with strained cheerfulness, 'Talk to him for his own sake.'

Sara thought, *It's all too late. What can I do?* At school she had never told on anyone and at home she had never ever told on Emily. *I've betrayed him, that's what I've done.*

She was so overwhelmed by this thought that from now on she divorced herself from the whole scene and acted dumb as if there was a screen between her and those three preying witches who sat before her under the guise of adults.

'Sara, this is a note of what you have been telling us. Would you be good enough to read it and sign it?'

'Why?'

Detective Sergeant Freeman smiled at her as he held out a biro. 'It may help us. We are carrying on a big investigation.'

So all the time he had been making notes. The net was tight now. Sara's eyes were too blurred to read the form properly but she soon gathered it was about everything she'd told them. She reluctantly took the pen and signed her name at the edge of the paper. Her writing was almost impossible to decipher. It was all she could think of doing.

When the police had gone Sara sat down on the floor in the corner of the kitchen. She hugged her knees and stared at the tiled pattern on the lino in front of her feet. Her cheeks felt hot, she ran her hands through her black hair that hung straight down in line with her drooping shoulders. She pushed hair over her face so she couldn't be seen. She counted the lino tiles through the strands of her hair as if they would give her a secret and magical number. *What have I said, what have I done?* she thought. *What will they do to him?* She tossed her hair back over her shoulders. One thing became more and more certain to her.

The Fuzz were after Liam, and they were after him because of what she had said. She sat there for about an hour until she could bear it no longer and stood up abruptly.

'I'm going to bed.'

Mum looked at her watch. 'Half past eight. An early night will do you good.' Sara pushed past her. As she ran upstairs, a car drove up and Emily came through the front door. How could she tell Emily about this? She banged the door of her bedroom and stood, trembling against it. She put her hands over her hot cheeks, walked over to the window and leaned out. If only Rubes was with her! In the damp dark she imagined their hut nestling on the downs. What was the time? Eight-forty. They were going to meet up there tonight - say *The Fuzz reach his house first?*

There was only one thing she could do. She closed the window, put on her anorak, opened her bedroom door quietly and stood on the landing. She could hear Mum and Emily talking in the kitchen, something about a hot drink. She crept downstairs and into the living room, and tiptoed over to the French windows. She turned the door handle as slowly as she could then walked quietly up the garden and climbed over the wall.

She felt better now she was acting. The tight circle in her mind broke, she was filled with a crusading spirit that submerged her feeling of guilt. She walked boldly, remembering how even as a small child she had not been afraid of the dark. One winter afternoon, when the sky was low and grey and the snow was coming, she had explored an empty house, all by herself, without any fear. She remembered looking out of the window of the house and watching the snow drift down into the wilderness of its back garden.

She thought of it because tonight up on the downs the sky was like that, low and grey and this time full of rain. Grass, houses and trees were only distinguishable by a change of tone, one layer slightly greyer than the others. Underfoot the grass felt damp.

'I'll go to the hut first,' she thought. He might have come early, had his tea and come over to wait for her. She peered in through the window. She could see nothing, only shadowy shapes. She rushed through the door and felt for the torch which they kept in a little box by the back wall. She flashed round the light but there was no-one around, only the old patchwork blanket, the two pillows, the fag ends to remind her of Liam. She went out, forgot to close the door, rushed back and pushed it tight, then ran back down to the main road towards his house.

Part two

Don't go asking
where I've roamed

Chapter seven

Running through the wind

'What are you doing ? I was just coming up to the hut. I told you never to come here.' Liam's eyes were bright, his lips thin looking, his skin pale through his unshaven stubble. His anorak was crumpled as if he'd been lying around in it, his jeans were torn at the knee. There was something glassy and edgy about the way he spoke. His dog, Tumbler - a small white-haired terrier, came through the hall wagging its tail at Sara but she ignored it and took hold of Liam's arm. 'It's awful!' Her breath came quickly and tears filled her eyes.

'You'd better come in. No-one's at home. The old man's up the pub and mum's with a friend.'

But there seemed as if there was no time even to cross the little hall into the sitting room so she stood where she was, out of breath, and told Liam everything that had happened so far as she could remember.

He shoved her off and spoke bitterly: 'I know what they're like. They've got a big case on and they're after me because I might be able to help them.'

He paced up and down the hall, rubbing his hands together nervously. Then he changed, his voice went softer, he held Sara gently.

'Don't you worry, I'll look after you. It was your mother, was she lit up or something? We have to get going, that's for sure, and we have to go together. You and I against the world! Stop looking so frightened, there's nothing to be frightened of. The Fuzz are sure to come round here so we can't stay and we can't go to the hut either, it's too near and there's all that stuff up there.'

Sara watched him with her heart in her mouth as he rushed through the house collecting up a few of his belongings and putting them in an army haversack his brother had left behind.

'I can't come,' she said, tears rolling down her cheeks.

His eyes were compelling. 'You've got to come, I can't do without you, you know that. Anyhow, you can't ever go back to that mother of yours.'

'She did it because of me.'

Liam laughed at her. 'Of course she didn't. She did it for herself – that's who she did it for. Don't be daft.'

'What do you mean, she did it for herself?'

'She was tired of you, wasn't she, she must have been or she wouldn't have called in The Fuzz.' He pulled at her arm. 'Come on, they're after us all right. We can't waste any more time.'

She stood still for a while and then he kneeled at her feet. 'Listen, Babe, I love you. If you don't come with me I won't be able to face life. That's the honest truth.'

She went pale. That was something she couldn't risk. She loved him didn't she? If she was responsible for his death she couldn't live with herself. Besides, he might be right. Mum had probably had quite enough of her. If she wasn't there Mum wouldn't have to worry about her all the time. Or would she – or would she worry even more if she wasn't there? *Not if there's no bad news. Not if she understands I'm saving Liam's life I could leave a message on the answer phone.* She felt in her pocket for her mobile, then remembered she had left it behind in her bedroom.

'Liam, I need to leave my Mum a message. Have you got your mobile on you?'

'What message?'

'Just to say I'm all right.'

He pulled his mobile out from his pocket and looked at her sharply. 'We've no time, be quick.'

She rang the number and hoped Mum was busy reading to Emily. 'I'm all right,' she recorded, 'I'll be all right. You don't have to worry.' And now there was no further time to think.

'That's my girl. We'll have to hide, you know that?'

'I don't know anything any more,' she said with her head down.

He pushed her long black hair through his fingers and kissed her lightly. 'I knew you'd stick by me, you're the only one, you know. You're the only one who can save my life.' He kissed her again. 'You will stay by me, won't you, Sara?' A faint challenge had crept into his voice. Sara looked up at him and spoke in a blank voice. 'Of course I'll stay by you, Liam.' She felt breathless from her huge commitment. *Nothing makes sense any more* she thought, *but I can't leave him if he'll-*

They stepped out together into the damp night - for now it had begun to rain – and she felt, for the first time, a sense of excitement and purpose. *She had betrayed Liam and now she was saving him.* Liam was pulling her closer to him, organising her, confiding in her, leaning on her. Without her he couldn't live.

'Where are we going?'

'Up the woods. We can spend the night up there. They won't get us up there.'

'But it's raining.'

Liam looked up at the low sky, then down at Sara's face. 'We're not put off by a bit of rain, are we? Not when they're after us.'

He held her hand tighter, and unaccountably they both began to giggle, quietly at first, then louder, then quietly again; and then they ran in silence, stumbling up the road and across to the fields that rose up to the downs. They sped across the grey, damp grass like hares running away from a pack of dogs. If Liam hadn't known the way they would never have reached the woods; for here, up on the downs and away from the road, everything was in darkness. Every now and again, they stopped to look back and watch car lights move in the distance, following the same curling pattern, the same road. As far as they could tell, no car had yet stopped outside Liam's house. They climbed up the slope, clinging to each other. The long grass dampened Sara's jeans from the knees downwards. Her discomfort grew and for the first time she wondered how it would all go, but only for a minute. After all, she should suffer some discomfort for what she had done.

They panted as they climbed up towards the pine wood.

The needles underfoot were soft and pliant and in many places dry. The smell of the trees in the rain was green and refreshing but there was very little light. Soon they came to a place where the rain did not reach their faces. Liam lit a match. They were surrounded by tall, straight, thick trunks. A long way up, the sky was a patchwork of grey in between black pine needles. A watery moon hovered behind the trees. The ground was dry and soft. The match spluttered out and Liam fumbled in his bag for a plastic groundsheet he had hastily packed. This was not the first time that he had run away.

'Brilliant!'

'That's not all,' said Liam. 'Takes brains, you know. What about this then?' He took out a crumpled piece of silver coloured sheeting. 'Space age stuff, specially made to keep out the cold.'

They lay down on the groundsheet and tucked the sheeting round them. In the great silence of the wood, Sara could hear the rain pattering down, the minute crackle and patter of night animals in the undergrowth. An owl hooted and Liam lit another cigarette. The little glow was a comfort, a hearth in the huge darkness.

'Don't you worry, Sara,' he said between puffs. 'They won't get us up here.'

Sara looked up at the fringes of dark grey sky. Sitting on the stone wall at home, she was used to country quiet, but now the vast sense of isolation overwhelmed her, and her hand reached out for Liam's. She was caught in a web of thoughts about home. What would Mum do when she found she had gone? What would Emily do? She turned over and whispered to herself: 'They won't care, why should they, they have each other. Anyway, there's Ben. I bet Mum phones him first of all.'

She was uncomfortable and wanted to sit up, only that meant disturbing Liam. So she turned over and snuggled up to him. After a long while his presence settled her spirits and finally lulled her to sleep.

When she opened her eyes again, the black grey sky between the high pines had paled to light grey. She stared, perplexed, imagining she must be in a dream. The sheeting had slipped off her, and although her anorak had kept her warm, her legs were stiff and cold and her hands were blue. She stretched out and yawned and then her thoughts tumbled into place. But Liam was not there though the mark of his body was still pressed into the groundsheet. She sat up and peered through the tall trees. They were densely planted and there was very little undergrowth between them, only a few straggling brambles and ground elder. As far as she could see the ground was covered with heaps of brown pine needles, so soft no-one would ever hear them. She screwed up her eyes. Was that a sandy path winding through the wood or the ground glinting in the first rays of the sun?

Liam stepped out from behind a tree and waved cheerfully at Sara.

'Needed a pee – it's always a good alarm clock.' The air was fresh and sharp and Sara shivered and rubbed her legs.

'It's freezing.'

Liam sat down beside her and pulled the sheeting over them both.

'Have a fag.'

She yawned and shook her head.

'Warm you up.'

'Will it really?'

'Course it will. Fire, isn't it?' So he lit her a cigarette and put it in her mouth and she puffed and pushed the smoke out without inhaling.

'I don't like it, Liam, it's making me feel sick. Look, I really do think I better go home now.'

He put his arm round her and looked at her closely. His bright green eyes were hypnotic. 'You promised, you know how much I need you and it's not just that. You won't feel good if you go back, I know you won't.'

'Yes, but-'

'Come on, Sara, pull yourself together. Don't forget we have a train to catch.'

She sighed and he kissed her gently.

'The sooner we get a move on the better. We don't want to get caught here, do we? I mean you're in it as much as I am now. You don't want them to pick you up, do you?'

Sara stood up, frightened. What would they do?

'Good girl, we've got to get a move on.' Liam looked at his watch 'It's a quarter to five. The train won't be long.'

Sara stretched and yawned. An enormous exhaustion weighted down on her body. 'Where are we going?'

'London, we'll try and join the others. It will be good to meet up with them again.'

She kicked at the pine needles with her trainers. Perhaps she should run back home while the going was good. It was as if Liam knew what she was thinking. He grabbed her waist and kissed her anxiously. His breath smelled of smoke.

'Come on, Sara, don't sell out on me. Ruby's up there, don't you want to see her?'

He was pale and shaking, but as he looked at her pleadingly, his green eyes glinted in the early sun and she was captured again. Of course she would stay with him, whatever was she thinking? Besides, it would be wonderful to be with Ruby.

Liam neatly folded the groundsheet and the nylon sheeting and shoved them into his haversack. He covered the cigarette butts with pine needles -there was scarcely a dent to be seen. Now the birds began to sing and Sara's spirits slightly lifted. Perhaps it was an adventure after all.

Liam went first. He quickly followed the sandy path to the edge of the wood. 'Come on, fast as we can. Don't want to get caught, do we?'

Sara looked into his face. She was bemused by his pallor, his slightly erratic breathing, his mildly unfocussed eyes. His determination led them on until halfway down the slope he fell down. Sara panicked. She leaned over him and felt the rise and fall of his chest. What should she do? What should she do? She sat down beside him, stroking his forehead and willing him to move, to open his pale eyelids and greet her. A train slid through the valley and she could dimly hear the chug of the engine. 'Come on Liam, wake up, wake up. We have to go.'

She wondered if this was the moment for her to escape. But she was too terrified to leave him alone and looked down into the valley for help. Was that a policeman down there? And that van, wasn't it a police van.? Would they come up the hill and find them?

'Liam, come on. Wake up, wake up, we have to go.'

She shook him and at last he opened his eyes. He struggled to sit and she propped up his back with her arm.

'Thought you were dying or something.'

His smile was half-hearted. 'One of those things. It happens like that sometimes.'

'We have to go,' she said urgently.

He stood up unsteadily, A little colour came back into his face and she put the haversack onto his back.

'Comes over me sometimes like that. Nothing to worry about.'

'I saw the train go.'

'Doesn't matter. Get the next one. Still very early.'

They went slowly down the hill and over the road, quickly, looking both ways and going when no-one saw them. They passed the churchyard that was behind a low wall, a little way from the church. Most of the graves were green, grassy mounds that had lost all identity. Liam pointed to the ground: 'I'm going to be buried here. I told my mum that the other day. It's the peace and quiet.'

Sara made her way through the long, wet grass, passing two very old yew trees that seemed to be curtseying to each other. She looked up at Liam.. Why was he thinking of death? He was too young and besides, without God it was best to forget about death. It was too final.

They went through a white, wooden gate that divided the churchyard from the allotments where new spinach, cabbage, kale and sprouts were growing, guarded by two scarecrows. One was made of sticks and straw, another was simply a white, torn piece of sheeting tied to an iron pole.

'Might need that!' Liam tore off the sheeting and stuffed it in the haversack. They both giggled.

They went over the wooden stile at the end of the allotment patch and along the thin overgrown path that led to the back of the station. The juddering noise of a train grew louder and louder and they broke into a run, through the nettles, through a gate in the palings and onto the end of the platform. The train drew in short of where they were. A guard was pacing up and down at the other end of the platform and when a man in a dark suit took his attention, they ran down towards the train and jumped into the first carriage.

'Keep away from the window!' whispered Liam.

As the train pulled out of the station they sat back stiffly in their seats, trying to regain their breath.

'Say they come round for the fare?'

'Got enough,' said Liam, patting his pocket.

Sara couldn't get rid of her anxiety. She looked out of the window and tried to calm herself by watching the familiar countryside give way to rows and rows of little houses. When Dad was around she had only ever gone to London for treats, maybe to see a show, a musical or a pantomime, or to look at the Egyptian Mummies in the British Museum, or to have a day at the zoo. The journey was never long, she and Emily played silly games and Dad talked about where they were going and what they were going to do as if it was the most exciting event in the world. She had felt secure and adventurous, and the memories of those outings had stayed with her like little gold bees who gathered honey for her. She was an eternity away from those times. Being with Liam wasn't like being with her family.But she loved him, didn't she? Or had he captured her? It was hard to tell.

'I'm longing to see Ruby,' she told him. Ruby was so different. They talked to each other and laughed and there was no sense of leaning on each other. Anam Cara, she whispered to herself, my soul mate.

'Yes, well, let's hope she's there.'

'Why shouldn't she be?'

He pulled a face. 'You never know if The Fuzz haven't cleared them out.'

'You mean, we might not see her?'

'I'm just saying you never know.'

She watched him taking some pills; she didn't ask him what they were. Was he more afraid than she was?

At Waterloo they used to go straight to the underground; they looped through those dark tunnels and magically arrived at their dream destination. Dad knew everything. He never made a mistake, unless dying could be called a mistake.

Footsteps, she could hear footsteps coming up the train. Liam shifted himself opposite her and gazed intently out of the window. 'Tickets, please,' said the man in uniform, not in a hostile voice but with a suspicious look at Liam. Sara's heart leapt into her mouth, her heart beat fast. She had always paid her fare upfront before.

Liam slowly turned round and nodded to the ticket collector. He drew a twenty pound note out of his pocket. 'We only just caught the train in time so we couldn't get tickets. That's for both of us.'

'Return?'

Sara waited to see what he would say. There was a pause.

'No, not return,' said Liam.

Chapter eight

Don't go asking

'I'd like to see Si before we go up the squat,' said Liam as he
shoved his ticket into the slot and swung through the barrier.
Sara followed him. She felt overwhelmed by the rush of people,
the electronic information boards, the little stores selling
accessories, the counters of baguettes and coffee, the shouting
and the shoving.

'I think he hangs out near here or he might be up the Dilly.'

'I want to get to the squat. Tower Hamlets, isn't it? I want to
see Ruby.'

Liam was barely listening. She knew he was already thinking
of his old life, his old mates, how they hung around bars and
picked up smack wherever they could. How up here he was free
of his father and his brother.

He's not listening to me any more, thought Sara, *he doesn't
seem to be the same person, he's going to abandon me any
minute.*

She kept worrying about Emily and Mum and Gran. If only
she'd brought her mobile or had some money. 'I'm going to get in
touch with my Mum.'

Liam quickly put his arms round her. 'Sorry, Babe, I've been
thinking of myself. It liberates me up here see? ' He drew her
close and kissed her in the middle of the crowd. 'Listen, Sara,
I mean it. I can't do without you. Don't think because I feel
liberated I don't need you.'

She nodded as if she went along with him. How could
she explain all her feelings about him, when they were so
contradictory?

'That's all right, then,' said Liam. 'Look, Babe, I've got
something for you.' They were near Smiths, people were coming
and going with books and papers under their arms. He stood
very near her and drew something out of his pocket. It was a

small purple box and at first Sara didn't open it.

'Go on, go on, open it,' he said.

It was a ring, a small diamond ring.

'What's this for?'

'A token,' he said, 'to keep us together.'

'Where did you get it from?'

'It was a spare one in the drawer.'

'You mean it was your mum's?'

'Well, she never put it on. I think she got it from an aunt or someone. She said I would have it one day when – you know – when I had a proper girlfriend like you.'

'But it's hers,' said Sara. 'I don't want it. I don't ever want it.'

Liam smiled. 'Well, Mum would like you to have it, I know that.'

Sara put it back in the purple box and handed it angrily to Liam.

'We don't need that to stay together,' she said, once more nagged by her negative feelings. She should be feeling happy and free, but instead she wanted to go home. Was she betraying him again?

Liam leaned over and kissed her. 'That was meant to be my little secret. OK then, I'll put it away for another day. I'm a bit disappointed though. I thought you'd be so thrilled.'

Seeing Sara waver he took out the ring again and tried to put it on her middle finger but it was too big. 'It doesn't fit,' she said sullenly, 'It never will. You keep it.'

He kissed her again, this time winning her over. 'Secrets,' he said, 'I like secrets. I thought you might be pleased with it.' He put the ring back into his pocket and holding her hand tightly he began to walk on. *He's walking fast like he does when he's trying to avoid someone.* She looked round at the thousands of people they were leaving behind. In front of them was the tall, gracious archway that led to the world outside the station. Steep steps led down to taxi ranks and subterranean walkways. She was taken aback by the size of everything and the endless flow of people, taxis, cars, buses. How could they ever make out in such a place?

'Liam, I still need to phone my Mum.'

He drew her close to him. 'Listen, Babe, things aren't so bad.

We've got to lie low for a bit, that's all. If you start phoning your Mum she'll ask where you are, and if you tell her that, you know what will happen?' His eyes were watching her from some deep green cavern underwater. 'I don't stand a chance, Babe, if you phone your Mum.'

She sighed. 'I just want to tell Mum I'm still all right. I'm not going to say where we are or anything like that.'

He kissed her. 'They can trace a phone call as easy as that. Listen, Babe, she knows I'll look after you. I told her so.'

Sara nodded. 'I suppose so.' Picking up her uncertainty Liam reached into his pocket for his mobile. 'I got an idea. We'll phone Ruby. She'll never grass on us.'

He was suddenly angry with his mobile and shoved it back into his pocket. 'Battery's run down. Left the charger behind.'

'Everything's run down,' said Sara, 'Everything.'

'Yeah, it is. Everything. You're right. Everything.'

'Well, I'm going,' said Sara.

Liam held on to her desperately, searched her eyes, lifted her long black hair, whispered in her ear as if he had a secret no-one else should know. 'Tell you what, we'll go back to the station and I'll phone Ruby. Do you know her mobile number?'

Sara nodded. She couldn't resist his little acts of kindness. They helped her not to leave him, not to betray him again.

There was a round booth of phones at the end of the station before platform One and Liam fed coins into the slot. A plump lady walked by, holding the hand of a little girl who was dressed in bright red. Her hair was divided into little plaits that stuck out all over her head.

Like Ruby! It would be fun once they were with her.

'No answer,' said Liam, retrieving his coins. 'Doesn't mean she's not there. Knowing Rubes she's probably fast asleep. Whenever I see her she always seems half asleep.'

'That's not the Ruby I know,' said Sara. 'She's always doing things.'

Liam shrugged. 'Listen, Babe, we'll go and get something to eat.'

They walked back through the station, past the red letterbox and found a place to eat. They joined the queue inside the shop, and as they waited Sara remembered the few times that she had gone to the chippy with Dad, then gone round to Gran's to eat fish and chips. *Wonder what Gran's doing. I hope Mum doesn't tell her I've gone.* Sara was standing next to the steamed-up window. She made a mark on it with her forefinger, a great big question mark. The child behind was amused by her drawing.

'Is it a fish caught on a hook?' he asked.

'It's a question mark,' she told him.

'Why?'

'I was wondering if I should write to my Gran or not. Have you got a Gran?'

The little boy shook his head and his mother held him back.

'I don't want little'un to start mucking around with graffiti.'

Sara turned back and followed Liam as he edged his way up the queue. *I'd better not write. They might trace it. Mum knows I'm safe, she knows I'm not on my own. That's what I'll do. I'll phone in about a week.'*

Liam turned round and smiled at her. 'Be nice to see Ruby again,' he said, 'This will keep us going until we've found the squat.'

'What about Si?'

'It might take too much time to find him. I'm not worried. Everyone knows Si. We'll soon find out where he's hanging out.'

They were now at the top of the queue. Sara hadn't realized how hungry she was! Liam bought bacon butties and chips and they took them outside and leaned against a wall to eat them. 'Safer in the crowd,' he said.

In front of them was an endless flow of people going up and down the station; purposeful, well dressed, intent, sure of what they were doing, where they were going. *Not like us,* thought Sara. *There's nobody who knows us.* It was like being invisible, two people who'd come up from the country whom no-one could see. Then things changed. Liam was bounding away from the wall with his mouth full of chips. He was waving to someone in the crowd. 'Si, Si!'

He was a very tall, thin man, a little older looking than Liam with a short black beard and fuzzy black hair. His skin was sallow and he wore a hooded green anorak and tight denims. He walked with a swagger, head and shoulders above most people. Liam bumped into him and in the course of a few seconds Si looked angry, startled, pleased.

'Hi, Liam, how amazing, I haven't seen you in a minute. You look whacked!'

Liam rubbed the side of his head. 'We're in the hot seat, Si. We're going up Tower Hamlets, meeting up with friends from home. Do you want to come?'

Si laughed. 'It's not the right weather, mate. I've got to stick around here. Who's this?'

Sara took a step backwards. She didn't feel safe in front of this tall, flamboyant man.

'Sara. My girl.'

'You baby snatching or something?'

' Of course not. You wanted to be with me, didn't you, Sara?' There was an edge to Liam's voice.

What am I doing here, why did I follow him? Must I always follow him because I gave his name to The Fuzz?

Sara hid behind her long black hair.

'This ain't no wild child,' said Si bending down and chucking Sara under the chin. She shook him off. 'What you in a muck sweat for?'

In a rapid, breathless voice Liam told Si what had happened.

'There's a always a first time,' he said, smiling at Sara, 'I ran off when I was younger than you.'

But I haven't run off, I'm just supporting Liam. Why can't I tell him?

Over the noise of the crowd there was the whine of a police siren. The police were spilling out into the station. Si pulled down his hood. 'See you later.'

Liam grabbed Sara's hands and ran with her to the underground. They ran down the steps and Liam bought tickets. 'They won't find us here,' he whispered, pulling Sara towards the District Line as if their lives depended on it.

'That was nothing to do with us,' said Sara, out of breath, feeling the weight of Liam's control.

'You never know with them,' said Liam. 'You can't take nothing for granted.'

At Bank they switched over to the Docklands Light Railway. 'Not far now,' said Liam, 'We get off at West Ferry.'

She knew nothing about this part of London. She might as well have been in another country. Then she thought of Rubes, the only one who understood her, and she followed Liam as if meeting up with Rubes again was her only chance of surviving.

Chapter nine

Bed's just a wooden floor

'Its huge, are you sure this is the right place?'

'Of course I am. I tell you what, they said the entrance is round the back, down the alley.'

Sara stared up at the huge brick building. Why was it empty? Who had left it there, open to tramps and squatters and anyone who needed shelter?

'It happens to lots of buildings,' said Liam, ' specially nowadays.'

They went down the alley to the right of the house, opened a tall wooden gate and walked round to the back of the building. The lower part of the brick work was covered with graffiti, yellow and red shapes looping their way under the windows. Liam pushed open a door and there they were, inside, in a dark passage, assaulted by a loud thumping of drums. Sara's heart beat fast at the sweet smell that drifted towards them. Was Ruby there? Were the others all lying around, smoking? Liam led the way down the passage and into a large room. Thin red curtains were almost drawn so everything was murky, but by the thin blade of light Sara made out a rusty mirror on the wall beside a torn print of a naked woman. Her eyes grew adjusted to the dim light and she looked round. The sofa and chairs were old and filthy and a dusty oil lamp stood on a rickety table beside a grey-striped mattress. Then her heart lifted and she ran forward.

'Hi, Hi Ruby,' she shouted over the cd player.

Ruby's dark eyes shone as she hugged Sara warmly. 'So you've come up at last. So good to see you, so good.'

They hugged each other again; then Sara held her friend at arm's length to make sure she hadn't changed much. Ruby was clean, heavily scented, wearing what looked like a man's blue shirt over blue jeans. Even in these clothes she looked glamorous, her hair clean and shining, her voice loud over the noise of the cd player. 'Can't tell you how good to see you at last. I tell you; I was wondering what was happening.'

'We're on the run,' whispered Sara into Ruby's ear. 'They're after Liam and it was all my fault, it was all my fault Rubes.'

They sat cross-legged on the floor, opposite each other, holding hands. 'Nothing's your fault,' said Rubes,' There's lots you don't understand , that's all. There's nothing your fault.'

Ruby's voice was rich, whether she was singing or speaking. It gathered Sara in, cradled her, soothed her, took away the burden she had been carrying around like a load on her back.

'Oh, Rubes, I can't tell you how good it is to see you,' she repeated.

'Hey,' said Ruby suddenly getting up, 'Come and meet Dave.'

He was sitting cross-legged on the sofa, his black curly hair bushing out over his shoulders, his thick, black, curly beard dwindling to a few bent strands. His shirt was unbuttoned, revealing a pale, hairy chest. His torn bleached jeans reached his calves and his feet were bare. He was reading a paperback with a lurid cover.

'Hi, Dave, remember me?'

'Hi! Good to see you.'

He smiled at Sara, then went back to his reading.

'Haven't you got more than that to say?' said Ruby, snatching the book from him.

'Not these days,' he said, forcing the book out of Ruby's firm fingers. 'These days I'm bent on escape,' He looked up and laughed.

Two other men came into the room.

'Hi,' said Steve.

Sara recognised his tall lumbering figure from the Boar's Head but she had never seen Pete before. He was small, with thin brown hair and sharp lines on either side of his mouth and a pale pitted skin.

He turned up the cd player until it was impossible to talk. Sara looked at Ruby – why was he cutting out all conversation? She peered round the room and fixed her mind on another picture pinned to the wall, the half torn face of a male singer she didn't recognise, tilted onto an orange and red background. Liam had shut his eyes and was swaying to the lyric as if he had forgotten Sara now they were here. Ruby pulled a face and over the battering rhythms Sara asked her if there were any rooms going.

'I'd say,' shouted Ruby, 'Never been in such a big squat before. Come on, Sara, let's get out of here. As a parting shot she raised her voice and sang along with the cd.

Ruby took hold of Sara's hand and led her through another door into the hallway, banging the door behind her.

'Now we can talk. I'll take you round and you can tell me what happened.' As they walked from room to room Sara told her everything, about how she wanted to phone Mum and how Liam was scared of The Fuzz. She could say anything to Ruby, she could trust Ruby with her life, she knew that. They climbed up the wooden stairs lined with iron-wrought banisters.

'This must have been a posh place in its time,' she said.

Ruby nodded. 'Sort of place I could have lived in as a princess.' She put on her princess pose. 'Sort of place where you had servants and they brought you food on a silver platter-'

'And people bowed to you,' went on Sara, laughing as she spoke, 'and everyone knew you.'

'Yes, everyone.'

When they were in the juniors they were singled out for the stories they told together, praised for their imagination and ability to work with each other. It's still a safety valve, thought Sara, somewhere to go when we can't quite take what's happening.

There were several empty rooms and plenty of mattresses around.

At the top of the house there was a flight of small steep stairs that reached the rooms under the roof.

'Me and Dave have one of these rooms,' said Ruby, 'It's quiet up here, ' she spoke like an actress, 'Far from the madding crowd.'

'That was the last book we read,' said Sara, 'and I agree with you. It's quiet up here, away from everyone. Except you.'

Ruby hugged Sara again. 'Come through here, I'll show you something.' They went into a room that was half demolished. The old yellow paper was partly stripped off the walls and the plaster had fallen off in chunks and lay round the room. The ribs of stripped wood showed up in places. The fireplace, that had once been finely tiled, was ripped to pieces and half the tiles lay broken on the floor. There was nothing at all in the room, only a dusty window that let in yellow, muzzy light, and two mattresses lying side by side in front of the fireplace. The only other fixture was a sink, cracked and yellow from disuse. One of the taps was missing and the rusty hollow tubes that remained were criss-crossed with little cobwebs. The ceiling was stripped to the beams and little bits of fluff and feather stuck out where birds had flown in through the cracks and nested.

'They'll be back in the spring ' said Ruby, 'singing for all their worth.' Then her expression changed.

'Anything could happen before then.' She suddenly looked deflated as if she could only envisage frightening things, not good things like the little birds.

'It's Dave,' she said, 'He's changing.' and she repeated, 'Anything could happen.'

Sara smiled and Ruby added in a light voice, 'Like Monsters coming up the stairs after us.'

'It's funny about monsters,' said Sara. 'When you're a small child you really love them, or at least they don't seem to be like monsters who have any power because all the stories tell you they'll always be defeated. Then when you get older you get frightened. I mean, they come in every shape and form, don't they? I was talking to Liam about the Minotaur.'

'The one who killed all the virgin maidens.'

'That's right.'

Ruby laughed. 'Well, at least the Minotaur won't want me.' She stood straight again and pointed to the sink.

'The water doesn't run in here or the two bathrooms. We all have to wash in the kitchen. We can't make out why there's water there. Maybe it's a different system and the guys before us paid for it somehow. It's awkward but we have a notice on the door to warn people.'

There was a little noise and Sara looked up to see if it was a bird returning to its nest.

Ruby shrugged. 'You'll get used it, Sara. You have to. These places are full of wild life, they always are. You learn to live with them. After all, they need a home as much as we do.'

'My mother's worst fear is rats. We had the rat man round ever so many times.'

'What about you, do you mind rats?'

Sara gave Ruby a look of grotesque horror. 'You know I do.'

'Call on me,' said Ruby, 'I'm not afraid.'

Sara took her hand. 'That's it in a nutshell, Rubes. You're not afraid of anything. That's why you experiment, just to see how far you can go. But I'm not like that, I'm a real coward. '

Ruby hugged her. 'That's not true. You're the brave one, Sara, not me. How many people would stick to a man because they'd betrayed him. They'd laugh it off. They wouldn't give a toss.' She paused for a moment and looked into Sara's eyes. 'All round you're much braver than me. About life, I mean.'

'Come off it,' said Sara, looking round the room. 'This will do me and Liam. Are there any blankets?'

'Follow me,' said Ruby. 'By the way, have you got any other clothes?'

Sara shook her head. 'Only what I'm wearing.'

They went out of the room and through a door that was lurching on one hinge. It was a small darkish room and the floor was covered with old army blankets, denim jeans and jackets.

'Where did all these come from?'

Ruby shrugged, 'No idea. We found them when we came. I should take what you want if you can find your size.'

Sara put her fingers to her nose.

'Is it the clothes that smell?'

'It's the room. The skylight's shut there's no air, I tried to open it the other day but I couldn't and I didn't want to break it. Here, try this on.' Ruby put some trousers up against Sara and they both burst out laughing.

'They'd fit a six- foot man!'

In a second Sara was back in school fooling about with Rubes at the back of the hall. Someone had left out the dressing- up box and they both put on funny, feathery, purple and orange hats and decided to wear them through the morning. They were rebels, even then, she thought.

She rummaged among the clothes and picked out a small pair of jeans. 'Hey, these will do!' She put them on and found a jacket and Ruby said they looked quite good.

'No underwear,' said Ruby, 'you'll have to keep washing it. I do. Hey – what about these for me?' She had picked up a pair of tight jeans and put them on.

'Really suits you. Wish I had a skinny figure like you.'

'What's wrong with your figure?' said Ruby, 'Anyway, it's best to take what you want while you can.' She poked around the dirty blankets. 'Here's two, it should be enough for the moment.' She looked up at Sara. 'Or do you want three?'

'I'm not that warm,' said Sara.

'Then take three. Here you are, put them in your room. You never know who's going to turn up and what they'll want. Lots of people come and go and most of them haven't got much.'

Sara went back to her room and put the blankets over the mattresses. She ran back to Ruby. 'So it's a well-known squat?'

'Is it! They come from all over. But it won't be forever, it won't be long before we're locked out.' Ruby couldn't hide her troubled look.

'Then what happens?'

'We'll stick together.'

'Yeah, we'll stick together.'

When they were at school they used to put their right hands together, palms facing each other, as a sign of solidarity. They did it now, spontaneously, in the musty room where they couldn't breathe properly, as if they would stand by each other forever.

Ruby dropped her hand. 'I'll show you my room now, it's really near yours.'

They went out onto the attic landing where there was one

more door to the left.

Inside, the window was open and the sun shone on a double sleeping bag and a wooden box propped up against the wall where Ruby put her make-up. There was a small rag rug on the floor by the box where they sat cross-legged, facing each other.

'It's a nice room ,' said Sara, 'but not as good as your house at home. Why did you leave it? Come to think of it, why didn't you come to the party?'

'I didn't want to let you down,' said Ruby, 'It was Dave. He was in touch with someone up here selling black dust for a song. He wanted me to go with him and we had an argument. In the end I gave in. I knew other people would go to the party and I didn't think it mattered that much me not being there.'

'It did,' said Sara, 'You know it did.'

Ruby hugged her. 'I know, I know. I felt awful really.' She started to pick at the rag rug and spoke with her head down, concentrating on the pieces of rag she was pulling out. 'There was another reason. There was this chick who wanted to start messing with Dave. I could tell from her expression and the way she sidled up to him, silly bitch. I just couldn't handle it, not now I was on my own and maybe homeless. Anyway we smoked as we argued, and after a bit not going to the party didn't seem to be a problem any more. Besides, I wanted magic dust as much as him.' She looked up. 'I can't help it, Sara. I'm hooked.'

'So am I.'

Ruby looked up. 'No, you're not. You're emotionally hooked. You only do it because of Liam.' She lifted her palm again and pressed it against Sara's. 'See, we're really close. If you need me in the middle of the night-'

'I know. And I'd do the same, Rubes. You know that, don't you?'

Ruby's eyes glistened. 'Of course I do. You don't have to say it,' She paused. 'It's just sometimes when I get high I change, like I did before the party. I don't mean, it Sara, it's just I can't help it.'

They hugged each other again and once more Ruby said she was sorry about the party.

Sara smiled. 'I know you are, you don't have to say it either.'

She looked round the room. 'Do you ever want to go home, Rubes?'

'Sometimes. But if Mum came back with her back-door man and paid the rent, she'd kick me out, I know she would. She's quite jealous of me really. So you see I wouldn't have anywhere to go. What about you?' Ruby's dark lustrous eyes searched Sara's pale face.

'I like being with you, but I'd like to go back as well. The thing is – I don't quite know how to put it.' She paused. 'It might be true to say I'm hooked on Liam or he's hooked on to me, or something. Half the time I don't know what I feel. The only thing I know is that I care about him enough not to leave him, and you being here makes all the difference. But I do want to go home, as well, I know that.'

Ruby laughed. 'Little home girl! You always were despite your Mum and that awful man of hers. There's no point thinking about it. You've chosen to be with Liam for the moment, so you're here , not there. You can't put the clock back. Now listen to me, Sara, we're going to light up here, while we can. We'll have fun, we'll do everything for the hell of it. Why not? We've nothing to lose.'

'I have,' said Sara, 'but there you go.'

'You're right,' said Ruby, her deep eyes suddenly looking solemn. Then they sparkled again. 'It's like taking time out, that's all, that's no bad thing. In this squat we all share everything, that's how it works, but we don't interfere with each other's lives.'

'I need to think straight,' said Sara, 'I haven't been able to think straight for ages, ever since Dad died. I don't know why I can't think straight any more.'

Ruby laughed. 'I've *never* been able to think straight. Or at least, I can't remember ever thinking straight. Maybe when I was a babe in arms and couldn't understand my mother. Once I understood her she screwed me up nearly all the time She never did want me, you see. She had me when she was about my age and she thought I'd ruined her life. That's why I started to go around with Dave. We understand each other, we have the same scars.'

76

'You're a warm, loving person, Rubes.'

'If I am I don't get it from my Mum. It might be from my Gran. She mostly brought me up. She was always singing, as if nothing in the world worried her. She used to make my clothes.'

'My Gran's a bit like that,' said Sara, 'Not that she sings, but she's sort of wise. She does make me laugh though. She wears these telescope glasses to watch the tele, and looks like something out of Dr. Who.'

She imitated the big glasses by rounding her fingers. Ruby laughed, then sighed. 'You're lucky to still have her. My Gran died suddenly and that was the end of all the fun.' She straightened her back. 'Until now.'

She looked round the room. 'It's not bad here. For one thing it's all free and at the moment the electricity's still on. We can't understand it, unless the lot before us paid for it. They must have known the ropes which is more than any of us do.' She laughed. 'Come on, I'll show you the kitchen.'

It was in the front of the house opposite the big room. There was a cracked butler sink, like the one in Sara's room, only here the cold water ran. Beside the sink was a wooden table and on it a camping gas stove with two rings. A small uneven kettle wobbled on one ring, a frying pan circled with congealed fat was balanced unevenly on the other. Beside the table was a sour yellow cupboard door. Inside there was a large packet of cornflakes, a tin of coffee, a plastic bag full of tea bags, a tin of powdered milk and six tins of coke.

'I'd love a cup of tea,' said Sara.

'You sound like an old woman!' Ruby filled the kettle with water and lit the gas.

'I'll make this for you and then see if the others want anything. Guys. They're dead lazy.'

'Can we get proper milk?' said Sara handing Ruby the old tin of dried powder. 'I don't mind shopping.'

'It depends if we've any sausage and mash.'

Sara laughed. 'Do you remember how we used rhyming slang at school so no-one would get what we were saying. We got that dictionary out, didn't we? Mind you, I've mostly forgotten it.'

'I don't use it much,' said Ruby pouring out the hot water into two cracked mugs. 'When I do hear it I think it's pretty so I use it but I've forgotten most of it too.'

'I'll go and ask Liam.'

'He's a funny one,' said Ruby, 'I can't quite get the hang of him.'

Chapter ten

Memories last to the end of day

Liam to himself:

It's good to sit here in a haze and dream of my heroes. No-one can get me here, no-one will interfere with my dream world. When I was very small Brad was my hero. I 'm four and he's riding his two wheeler up and down the road. Mum tells him to go indoors while she's shopping, and to look after me. He never listens to her. He doesn't need to. He's daring, HE CAN DO ANYTHING. It's a wet day, and we start off in the living room. The minute the front door shuts Brad says we've got to go outside and I've got to watch him and I've got to warn him if any traffic comes. I like it when he tells me what to do. I feel needed. This time he doesn't ride his own bike. He wheels Dad's bike out of the garage. It's a racing model, red and blue and white and shiny. 'You can't take Dad's,' I say.

"Course I can,' says Brad reaching up for the handlebars. 'He won't half be cross.'

'He won't know,' says Brad, 'If you tell him I'll cut off your left ear.'

He looks as if he means business so I put my hand up to protect my ear.

"Course I won't tell on you,' I say. I keep my hand over my ear until we're outside.

The rain skids across the road flipping and bouncing so there's a little haze above the tarmac. Brad's turning and leaping on the bike, as if it was a horse, neighing on two hooves. He's like a cowboy taming his mount. This goes on for a long time, me watching and him riding. Then I hear a car coming and I shout out, but the rain's noisy like a drum and by now Brad is round the corner. The car's red, like my toy car I had for Christmas, it's coming towards me, its windscreen wipers are going from one side to the other, fast as the car. The driver sees me and swerves. He nearly nicks my toes off. I run along the pavement shouting to Brad who's round the next corner. But the car's going too fast and the next thing I hear is Dad's bike scraping the road. I turn the corner. Brad's down there with his bike, shouting and screaming at me. 'I told you to look out for me, you little-'

A neighbour comes out and I am taken in. Through the lace curtains I see the ambulance arrive and then I hear a man's voice speaking on the telephone. I start to cry and the lady gives me a glass of milk and three jammy dodgers. She looks worried.

She says my Mum and Dad will be going to the hospital. The jammy dodgers stick in my mouth but I eat them because it's better than crying.

It takes a long time before Dad comes for me. I can feel the anger in the clutch of his hand. He's smiling at the kind lady, he's thanking her, but all the time he's almost breaking my wrist. Outside it's dark and he drags me angrily down to our house.

'How dare you go out in the rain when I tell you not to! Poor Brad, he wouldn't be in hospital if he hadn't been looking for you. He even took my bike so he could find you quickly. You don't deserve a brother like him. You could have killed him, that's what you could have done.'

I look up into his fiery green eyes. 'Dad, it was Brad's idea.'
'Don't you lie to me!'
'But-'
'I don't want to hear from you again, do you understand? Never.'
'But-'
He clipped me over the ear and dragged me home. He told me to go upstairs and not to come down until he said so.

After two days he came in and pushed me out. If Mum hadn't secretly fed me I don't know what I would have done.

When I went downstairs to the living room Brad was sitting in the brown armchair with his arm in a bandage. He smirked at me and I knew there and then there was nothing I could do, nothing at all. During those long lonely hours upstairs I had already begun to wonder if it had been my fault, if I had wandered out in the rain on my own. I had nothing to do up there and that's all I could think of. Was I to believe my hero or myself? I didn't know for a long time, I don't even know now. I know what it did to me though, it took away my sense of – how can I put it- reality I suppose. I don't much like reality. And underneath it all I'm angry, I'm still angry with Brad. He may have been right and I may have been wrong, but he never cared about me, not really. I'm angry with all the world.

'Wake up,' said Dave, 'Your girl's here. She's been listening to your muttering, haven't you, Sara?'

'I always listen to Liam's stories. Do you want a coke?' she asked him.

'All right.'

'I'm hungry,' said Sara, 'Afterwards we could go out and get something to eat.'

'What you talking about?' Liam stood up unsteadily and scuffed the side of Sara's head. His eyes were bright and dilated. He spoke breathily, in a rush. 'Look, we all share things here, everything, don't you see? We don't go off on our own and buy ourselves something when we're hungry. We don't do things like that.'

'I didn't mean, I didn't know-'

Sara stood in front of him, rubbing her head. She had never seen him angry like this before.

'Leave off,' said Dave to Liam. 'She'll know another time. Won't you, love?' He came over and gently chucked her under the chin.

Liam glared. '*You* leave off.'

'What's got into you?' said Dave, 'You was stoked a minute ago, what's the matter with you? You had a bad dream or something?' He turned to Sara, 'Tell you what, I'll go out and get some food. I got money in the kitty today.'

'Dealing?'

Dave nodded 'Won't be long, you two have a rest.'

Liam pulled Sara outside into the hall and upstairs to their room. It was still filled with dusty yellow light.

81

'Hey, that looks comfy.' His voice had changed. He didn't want to quarrel, he said as he gently pushed her down onto the mattress. He kissed her and stroked her hair. 'I didn't mean to hurt you,' he whispered in her ear as if he was revealing a secret no-one else should know. 'It was the last thing I wanted to do. I'm anxious, that's what it is, baby. You must understand. I'm anxious, under the influence.'

He tried to take off her jacket, but she pushed him off and sat upright, looking round the dusty, yellow room. 'I can't help being hungry,' she said.

'Dave will get something for supper. You'll see.'

'I want to go home.'

Liam sat up beside her. 'It's like I said, you can, but not yet. I'll tell you something now, Sara, so you'll understand more. I'm not meant to tell you but I will because I love you.'

He sounded as if she was the only one in the world who mattered. Maybe he really hadn't meant to hurt her. Maybe it was one of those things.

'What then?'

'Well, The Fuzz are after me because I'm involved in something quite big – it's called Operation Jenny.' He stroked her cheek and looked at Sara with a slight air of pride.

'What do you mean?'

'A big haul - they've got wind of it – they hope I'll lead them to it.'

'Is Si part of it?'

Liam laughed. 'Si's always part of it, He's a big candyman.'

'What do you mean?'

'Pusher. If he comes round here it's because he needs to lie low.'

Liam pushed back her hair – 'So you see, Sara, it's not the time to phone your Mum. No-one, no-one at all must know where we are – just for a bit.'

Sara stood up and went over to the window and scrawled a word in the dust.

'What are you writing?' asked Liam.

'Nothing.' Sara stared dreamily at the dusty word.

He lurched off the bed to read it but Sara scuffed it with the side of her hand.

The smell of fish and chips wafted up to the attic. Liam stretched back on the bed but Sara raced down two steps at a time. Ruby and Dave had bought a packet for everyone.

'Smells really good,' said Sara, sitting down on the threadbare carpet next to Ruby. 'Where did you find them?'

'Ma Patty up the road. She gives them to us in exchange for cokey. She's on the needle all right. Her partner's kicked the habit and keeps the business going. Mind you, he still likes his Lebanese gold.'

'What's that?'

'Hashish, leaves of Indian hemp.'

'You were always a one for words,' said Sara. She felt comforted by Ruby's warm presence. Even Dave was looking at her sympathetically.

'Listen, Sara, don't take no notice when Liam scuffs you. He doesn't mean it. It's when he's angry inside, that's what makes him do it. That's why he's always going round the jam house. He needs to forget. That's why he's upstairs now, blowing his mind out. He prefers that to fish and chips.'

Sara nodded.

'Doesn't he ever get hungry?' said Pete. The sharp lines round his mouth softened as he spoke. 'By the way, I got a birdseye – should do all of us for tonight.'

'See?' said Ruby proudly to Sara, 'See how we all share.'

'That's right,' said Dave, smiling intimately at Sara, as she ate the fish and chips with her fingers.

Chapter eleven

My soul's hungry

It was a cold, cheerless spring day. Liam pulled at the sash cord and the window clattered right down.

'It's freezing,' yawned Sara, snuggling under the dark, grey army blankets. Liam tried to lift the window again, but each time it slipped back. Sara sat up with the blankets huddled around her.

'Nothing works in this house.'

'What do you expect? The bloody Ritz?' He laughed.

'Can't you make it work?' She pushed her tangled hair away from her eyes.

Liam struggled again and this time managed to secure the window on the hook. He looked round critically. 'It's filthy in this room. We should sweep up.'

'There's no brush.'

Liam sat down on the mattress. He pulled the blankets away from Sara but she tugged them back again.

'Come on, dozy.'

'Nothing to get up for.' Sara felt in her bag. She kept it close to her at the side of the mattress. She took out her comb and scraped at her knotted hair. Strands of lighter brown showed at the roots but there was nothing she could do about it now. They sat in silence for a few minutes as Liam carefully rolled a cigarette, lit it and handed it to her, then rolled another one for himself. They smoked in silence. Sara was going to stub out the cigarette on the floor beside the bed, but something stopped her. She stood up, wrapped in blankets, and threw the stub into the fireplace. She went over to the window.

It was one of those spring days that took a step back to winter. The birch tree on the right of the window looked grimy as if the city smoke had etched itself into the trunk. Little buds

85

were pushing out bravely. Sara felt a fellow feeling for the tree. Surely it was like herself, longing for sunshine. She turned round and sank down on the mattress next to Liam. He had lit up again and this time was smoking dangerously close to the blankets.

'Hey! Careful! We don't want to set the place on fire.'

Liam grinned inanely. 'Why not, why don't we want to set the whole bloody place on fire? I don't mean that. I was remembering when I was six. It all started when Mum was lighting a log fire in the grate and a spark flew off and smouldered on the armchair. I was spellbound by the way fire could spread and start a new little fire somewhere else. I thought perhaps that's how the stars multiplied, catching fire from each other and after aeons of time, lighting up the whole universe.'

He stubbed the butt of his cigarette on a piece of rolled up newspaper.

Sara felt afraid. 'What you playing at, Liam?'

A brown hole was growing into the paper like an autumn chrysanthemum. She watched, mesmerised. Just before the flower broke into flame he smothered it with another piece of torn newspaper.

'What did you do that for?'

'Just to see how far I could go. If you're going to get anywhere in this world you have to understand the edge of danger.'

'We're not getting anywhere in the world,' said Sara, 'Anyway, I want to go home.'

Liam rolled to one side, got up and pulled her up next to him. He held her tightly, his green eyes mesmerised her. 'What you talking about, going home? Only cowards go home. Cowards don't face the edge of danger. You're frightened, aren't you, aren't you?'

She tried to pull herself free but he held her tighter. 'How many times do I have to tell you, they'll lock me up if they find me. Why don't you understand?'

He pulled her back onto the mattress. 'Let me tell you a bit more about Operation Jenny, then you might understand better. It's Si, he's at the centre of all of this.'

'All of what?'

'There's a gang of pushers who sell to the dealers. They can get whatever they want, wherever they are. They have links with the boats coming in. There was a deal a few days ago. The Fuzz are after them and they want me because I'm in with them. I'd be for the slammer, that's for sure. Now listen to me, Sara, don't you start stone-walling me. These people are my friends, see. I don't want to let them down anymore than you want to let me down. That's what it's about, lots of us, all in it together. Do you get me now?'

Sara stood up abruptly. What had she got herself into? She couldn't be loyal to people she didn't know. That was up to Liam, not her. But he was part of it and if she broke away she'd be breaking away from him. He was pleading with her, he really meant it, if she spread the word about where they were hiding out, that would be it. They would all be caught, Si and Pete and Dave and himself and-

She put her hands over her ears and Liam shouted at her, 'And don't you forget Ruby. She's meant to be your friend, isn't she?'

She hated it when he shouted and she ran downstairs. She began to cry. She didn't mean to be here but she couldn't get away either. She wouldn't let Ruby down, ever. Ruby was her soul mate.

What was she to do? She would have a wash in the kitchen, at least there was water down there. She felt the need to scrub herself so clean she was no longer contaminated by all this confusion and fear.

On her way she peered through the open door of the living room.

Dave was lying flat on his back, his mouth open, his black curly hair half over his face. Next to him was a girl Sara had never seen before. She was sitting up, staring ahead, her long fair hair loose over her thin shoulders. The floor was littered with dirty coffee cups and empty bottles of vodka and dirty syringes and cigarette stubs. A sweet, musty smell hung over the room like a dirty dishcloth, that's how she thought of it. Pete was on his mattress, still as the dead, grey sloping eyes closed so tight they looked as if they were sealed. It looked as if he'd had a bad hit. Where was Ruby? Oh God, there she was in the kitchen, sprawled out on the floor, legs under the table, head against the wall. Sara shook her but Ruby didn't come to, she was breathing heavily like an old man. What had she been on? Acid? Coke?

Sara jumped. It was Liam behind her, putting his hands on her shoulders, breathing into her ear.

'A bad scene, that's all. She'll come round. When you've washed I'll shift her into the living room with the others.'

'We'd better get a doctor.'

He thumped her shoulders. 'Don't you understand anything? We can't get a doctor.' Sara began to cry again and Liam softened. 'Look, don't you worry, she'll come round, they always do.'

'How do you know?' He looked at her vacantly. ' Promise you she'll come round.'

It was hard to wash with Ruby lying there like that but she did her best. Then she went out of the house and Liam followed her. Wouldn't he ever trust her? Would it never again be like old times?She was pale and stiff as if something in her heart and mind stopped her from moving normally and she was riding an invisible moving escalator that took her in one direction only.

They passed a café with a little notice in the window. *"Part-time Waitress Wanted"*

'Why not try?' said Liam.

Sara nodded. Anything was better than the squat. She liked the look of the small, friendly Italian but he took one look at Liam and became wary. 'The position is already taken. You go somewhere else.'

They walked on in silence side by side. Was he spying on her or did he want to be with her?

'Them wops. You can't trust a word they say.'

'It would have been a good job.'

In the past few days she had often been hungry. They had moved away from the routine of meals. Instead they bought a loaf or a bottle of milk and consumed it on the spot. One day there was nothing at all to eat because Steve had spent all the readies on coke.

'We'll share the coke,' he had said, and they had had a blinder. Sara looked up at Liam as they walked along. He was fragile as glass. How much longer could he go on like this? As if he could read her thoughts he reached out for her hand. 'I love you, Sara, you know that. Promise you won't leave me. Not yet.'

They walked on in silence until Liam stopped and cupped her face in his hands and gently kissed her.

'I got an idea. Let's go up Russell Square. The sun's coming out. We can get sandwiches there. Do you know it? When my Mum was in the National Hospital, I always used to visit her.'

My Mum's never been ill, thought Sara. I wonder what she's doing now, at this very minute?

In her mind she could see her mother with her arms full of daffodils, her calm, grey eyes looking straight at her. She could even hear her praying.

'Don't you think it's all right for me to phone my Mum now?' she pleaded, but Liam took her arm.

'Soon as The Fuzz have laid off thinking about me it'll be fine. Promise you that. It won't be long now.'

But any time seemed too long for Sara, and the same words rolled through her head over and over again. *Does Mum ever think about me, does she ever talk about me, does she wonder where I am, does Emily miss me?* And more darkly, *It must be peaceful now I'm not there, just Mum, Emily and Ben of course.*

She was suddenly desperate to see them, and as if he knew what she was feeling Liam grasped her arm and smiled at her. 'Listen, Babe, it won't be like this forever. I'll get back to having a job, and then we'll have some money to buy things.'

'You mean magic dust.'

'Of course I do. It's a good way of life. It doesn't stop you getting on.'

'Of course it stops you getting on.'

'That's a myth, it doesn't have to.'

They took the tube to Tottenham Court Road and walked down the wide, dusty subway, where a man was scraping a violin. Liam led Sara down Great Russell Street, round the back of the

British Museum and on into Russell Square. Her eyes lit up at all the pigeons.

'Aren't they pretty!'

'Scavengers, more like it.' Liam looked round. He kicked at the pigeons and they rose in a cloud of feathers.

'The café used to be on the other side,' Liam looked round anxiously. 'Unless it's gone.'

Suddenly the sun came out and impulsively Sara sat on a bench and lifted her face to the sun. Liam sat beside her and began to tell her of the last time he was here, five years ago now. Sara sometimes wondered if the past meant more to him than the present. He was often poetic about the past but drugs had brutalised him, she knew that now.

'I was about thirteen when Mum fell ill. It seems like yesterday. She had to come up here for tests and sometimes they kept her in because she was sick all the time and they couldn't make it out. There was a lot of hanging around, I remember that, but I felt free as well, there was no-one who knew me and I was off school. I used to wander off into this square and this is where I met up with Si again. I never thought I'd see my old school mate up here. He came over to me and I suppose I was flattered because he's older than me and hadn't forgotten about our friendship. Then one day when Mum had to stay in I didn't go home, I stayed around with Si.'

'What happened?'

'He showed me where he dossed down and said if I wanted a sleeping bag I could stay.'

Sara's eyes were blinded by the sun; in this flood of light she pictured Liam reading the story from a book.

Si lit a candle – a thick round one that was stuck into a bowl. It flickered on the table and I felt as if he had stepped back in time. I remember Si, tall and broad, sitting like a king in his highly coloured jacket and trousers, gently smoking with a peaceful expression on his face.

'A lot of people don't know how to make out,' he said, between puffs and indrawings of his breath. 'I discovered a long time ago

there's a mint to make in Adam.'

'What's Adam?'

'Ecstasy. All the kids want it, all of them. What's a party without Disco- biscuits? They need it and I can supply it. They pay me more than I pay for it, and that's what you call business. You don't even need an application form. You don't need nothing but your wits about you. How do you feel about that, Liam?'

'I dunno.'

Si put down his joint and opened a drawer . 'Watch this.'

He took some heroin and placed it in a careful line on a piece of silver foil. He went over to the candle and held the foil above it until the heroin became liquid and gave off curls of smoke. He handed me a tube and told me if I inhaled it would be like heaven.

I hesitated so Si inhaled it himself. 'I've had the habit for three years now, and I haven't looked back once.'

Would it stop me looking back, I thought. 'Would it stop me thinking of Brad and my so-called father who's never there when he's wanted anyway. Then I thought of Mum...

'I've got to get back to my Mum tomorrow.'

Si nodded. 'Tell you what, try dope. You'll be all right tomorrow with that. As a matter of fact they use it in hospitals for people with neurological diseases. Your Mum might be on it already, who knows?'

'OK then, if she's on it, I'll have a go,' said Liam.

The room became not just a shadowy cave but a treasure house. The scratched mirror on the right hand wall reflected the subdued colours of the floor; brown, ochre, grey, with stains like patterns dribbled onto a a thick page. The drawn green curtains made from dyed hemp wafted in the glass like the sides of a medieval king's tent; the two knives glinting by the sink turned into short swords waiting to be picked up and aimed; the cups were chalices so rare they were unique. Their silver handles gleamed like the magic half-circles I had once read about in his book on wizards. A half-circle was more powerful than a closed one, it was open to the energies that lay in the earth and sky. The cracks were ornate patterns beautifully sculpted in the silver, containing secret messages for those who drank out of them. I staggered towards the cups but sat down again. I felt sick but was still enchanted. After a while Si made up a bed under the table. 'Spare sleeping bag always comes in handy,' he said. 'Here's a cushion.'

The next morning seemed cold and depressingly grey as if there was nothing left of the party but a pile of fag ends.

'You can come as much as you like,' said Si, as I stepped out of the door. 'I'm mostly around in the evenings.'

Liam was silent for a while and Sara held his hand. Then he kissed her. 'I always did what I could for my Mum – the next morning I was back with her even though I felt awful. That's why she does what she can for me now.'

'What was wrong with your mum?'

'In the end they diagnosed MS. A mild form. You wouldn't know except for the stick. She mostly walks with a stick. That stick whips my dad up into a fury. He hates to see anyone weak, that's why he hates me.'

'You're not weak, you just do your own thing.'

'That's what my dad calls being weak.'

'Lucky to have a dad.'

'No I'm not, my dad's a killer.'

Sara pushed him away. 'How can anyone think that?' But Liam was following his own train of thought again.

'Then Mum had another bout in hospital and I went with her, only this time when I left her I went up the Dilly - that's where Si told me he was hanging out. It was good to have a friend around and quite often I didn't go home at all but stayed with Si. By the time Mum came out of the hospital I was hooked on the whole scene. It seemed such a brilliant way out. You see, all that time I never knew if Mum would pull through and if she didn't I would be at the mercy of two bullies. I forgot all about that when I was with Si.'

He went on reminiscing while the sun soaked into Sara's face. She let his voice drift over and around her, his memories like a strong and invisible thread that bound her to him. Then, suddenly, Liam started up, and abruptly pulled Sara to her feet. A little way off she saw a couple of officers questioning two men.

'That's nothing to do with us. What's the matter, just when everything was nice?' It was at that moment she saw a familiar figure, a little way down the path, turn round and wave to her and then disappear in between the trees. Surely it couldn't be Dad?

'What's the matter with you, seen a ghost or something?' said Liam. 'Come on.' He dragged her by the coat sleeve, along the way they had come. She was angry and tried to break loose and run back, but he gripped her tight. *Say it had been Dad, say he had been looking after her?*

'What's got into you?' said Liam impatiently. Sara didn't answer. She looked back again, over her shoulder. Nothing had changed. The same people were about, others were disappearing into the distance.

Liam swung round and spoke very emphatically. 'We'll go back to Tottenham Court Road and I'll buy you a steak.'

'Yes, but-'

Perhaps she was wrong. After all, she didn't believe in ghosts. Perhaps it was one of those illusions you have when your soul is hungry to see someone you love or when you're just plain hungry. The thought of a steak was irresistible. It was something she often dreamed about, a rich, juicy steak in a homemade gravy.

Maybe Liam had more up his sleeve than she had come to believe, maybe he would give her a good time after all, enough to make her forget the tall familiar figure with the intimate smile.

Chapter twelve

I've got no home

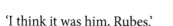

'I think it was him, Rubes.'

Sara was sitting on the floor opposite Ruby who was making herself up , peering in the little mirror to make sure her eye make-up went on in just the right way to enhance her brown glowing eyes. She turned towards Sara, holding up the thick brown eye pencil.

'But how could it have been? Or do you believe in ghosts?'

'No,' then uncertainly: 'It was something about his walk.'

Ruby applied her bright red lipstick in the same careful way. 'Lots people walk the same way. We're not all totally different, you know.'

'Do they? Walk in the same way I mean.'

They both jumped up and started to imitate different walks, laughing out loud as they tripped from one end of the room to the other.

'This is how drunks walk.'

Sara swayed from side to side and lolled her head about. Ruby laughed and demonstrated the walk of a man who was out of his mind. 'It wasn't like this, was it?'

They sat down again and Sara shrugged her shoulders. 'Anyway, why should my Dad's ghost be in London?'

'It's easy to make mistakes,' said Ruby shaking out her curly hair. 'I once followed a man all round thinking he was Dave. I think I just wanted him to be Dave, that's all.'

It was Liam's anger that made Sara afraid, made her stay in bed and sleep as long as she could. He was getting more and more of a control freak, and every time she tried to have a mind of her own he pinned her down in his anger, a butterfly he wanted to collect. Every day he reminded her that she had already got him into trouble and made her swear to make no phone calls and to stay in hiding with him. 'Or else-'

She felt weak and powerless and afraid, especially when he was bullying her into submission. To withstand his abuse she too began to take whatever drug was to hand. At first she didn't think it mattered because she was still trying to stay outside their circle. Every night Dad's voice told her that what had once been unthinkable could become habitual and however much she was tempted she must try to stay clean. But she couldn't, not at the moment. She had too much to bear. Her only other refuge was sleep so she'd go upstairs before Liam or any of the others.

One night she dreamed of Dad. He was waving to her from the other side of a very busy road, smiling, indicating he was coming across. Anyone could see how dangerous it was so she shook her head. He still came, dodging the cars, smiling, always smiling. And then a yellow sport scar screeched behind him and swooped him up on its low bonnet where he lay motionless, bleeding. She woke up in a sweat. Was it true he was looking for her? She slipped her feet onto the floor beside the mattress and stood up with difficulty. If only she'd brought her mobile. If only. But things had happened so quickly she hadn't remembered to bring anything at all. Ruby had lost her mobile and Liam made sure his never worked. There were still a few phone boxes around in this area and perhaps Ruby would come with her. It was difficult to know. Ruby loved her, she knew that, but she was always with the others, more and more deeply involved with a world no-one else could see or touch. Maybe it would be easier to forget the real world and go on getting high together, understanding each other in a way that no-one else could.

A few days later things came to a head. Dave had stolen some meat from a butcher's and gave it to Sara to cook. It wasn't very easy in the small frying pan and while she was cooking the joint of beef, she talked to Ruby. 'We'll have to eat with our fingers!'

They both laughed and reminisced about school dinners, and how half the time they bunged the cardboard food in a tissue and sluiced it down the loo. They danced round the room imitating what they had done. Sara was so caught up in the dancing that it was only the burnt smell of the meat that made her rush back to the cooker. Liam stormed in, picked up the frying pan and flung it on the floor in front of Sara. Fat spurted up and burned Sara's leg.

'Serve you right,' shouted Liam, 'You ruin everything, you do.' He swore at her and punched her in the face, hard on the cheek. 'Just because I was looking forward to a proper meal for once. Just like you to be a careless cow,' he roared out, shouting all the way up the stairs.

Ruby knelt down and examined Sara's burns. 'I think we need a doctor.'

'No we don't, it's not that bad. It's him that's bad.' Sara was crying uncontrollably.

Ruby held her tight. 'Don't you cry, Sara. Dave's like that. Angry. Take no notice. He was hungry, that's all.'

'We've nothing,' sobbed Sara, 'nothing to help my bruises or burns. I can't stand it any more, Rubes. I'm going home to my Mum.'

'I'll come with you.'

'Will you really?'

Ruby gave Sara a warm hug. 'There must be somewhere better than this.'

'I thought you liked it here.'

'I like getting high. I'll miss that.'

'I'll have to phone first.'

Ruby rushed upstairs and brought down their anoraks.

Outside it was raining and the dark wet pavement was streaked with orange reflections from the lamp light.

'Hey, you,' said Ruby, 'it looks as if the rain's running down your face. Can't you stop crying?'

Sara shook her head. She was shivering, in a panic.

'I've got some change,' said Ruby, when they reached the phone box. Sara calmed down. It seemed out of place in this street, but something people might have fought to keep. She knew that sort of thing happened because once Mum signed a petition to keep the Victorian pillar box up the road. Maybe in this street there were fans who were determined not to let the old phone box go.

Sara wiped her tears on her sleeve and tried to make her voice sound normal. Now the time had come it all seemed so simple. She lifted the receiver and put in the coins. Why hadn't she done this before? Why hadn't she done it weeks ago?

The phone rang and rang, but the answer phone was off and there was no voice at the other end. Sara started to cry again and Ruby took hold of the receiver.

'Did you dial the right number?'

Sara's voice struggled up from her throat. 'I never forget my home number. It's like a code to my old life, know what I mean? But something's wrong. Something's happened.'

Ruby raised her eyebrows: 'Like what?'

Sara clicked the rejected money back through the coin holder. She was suddenly angry. 'She's blocked me off, that's what she's done. They've all gone to Australia. I wouldn't put it past any of them. I should think my mum was glad to go.'

'Don't be an idiot. Of course she hasn't gone away.'

'You could see it coming a mile off.'

'You always imagine something stupid,' said Ruby, 'She might be looking for you.'

'Of course she's not!' Sara's anger subsided. 'I'm out of my mind,' she sobbed, 'Of course I can't go back. They wouldn't want me to.'

A picture of Dad slipped into her mind. He was walking her to school, his hand was warm and comforting and every so often he squeezed her fingers.

'I hate Ben, I'm never going back now, Rubes. Never.' Her voice gathered strength.

'You don't know,' said Ruby.

'She's never out at night.'

Ruby took out a tissue and wiped Sara's eyes. 'Come on. We've got each other. In the morning you'll wonder why you had such silly thoughts about your Mum. She loves you, she really does. Tell you what, we'll go and have a drink, just you and me.'

'I haven't any money.'

Ruby swung her scarlet bag into the air. 'I have.'

They went along arm in arm. Sara was still crying.

'Nothing to cry about,' said Ruby, kindly. 'We can try again.' For a while they walked on in silence; then Ruby said, 'I'll miss you when you go.'

'I thought you were going to come too.'

'I haven't got a family like you,' said Ruby, 'My mum would run a mile if she thought I was coming back.'

Sara turned to her. 'You could be part of my family. I mean, we are like sisters, aren't we?'

Ruby laughed. 'If we told people we were sisters they'd raise their eyebrows, wouldn't they? Like this?'

Sara laughed. 'You know what I mean.'

'Honestly, Sara, you're so naïve. Can you imagine your mum taking me in. It's the last thing.'

They walked in a silence for a moment. 'No,' said Rubes, 'The only way I can make out is up here.'

Sara looked hard at Ruby. 'You fit in more than me. Sometimes I get fed up with London. All these streets.'

They turned into the pub and found themselves in a lively, homely room full of noisy conversation where yellow and red lights splashed the walls with warm stains and a silent television showed scenes from a soap. 'I'm tougher than you,' said Ruby going through her bag. She made for the counter and Sara followed. Two old men were leaning on the shining wooden bar, arguing and laughing as they drank their beer. Ruby pushed her way through.

'You eighteen?'

Ruby laughed. 'Don't be insulting, of course I am. Want my identity card?'

'We have to ask,' said the barman who seemed scarcely older than Ruby. 'Rules is rules.'

'Two halves,' said Ruby swiftly, in case he wanted evidence of her age, 'and a packet of Walkers salt and vinegar.'

They sat down at a small table and looked at each other knowingly.

'To us!' said Ruby.

Sara clicked her glass against Ruby's. 'Forever!'

They drank quickly as if someone might come in and haul them into a police car. Ruby spoke quietly. 'There's one thing, Sara. In the end you'll find it easier to escape than any of us.'

'I've given up trying,' said Sara, clanking down her glass and scraping back her chair. 'Come on, let's get going, before they find us out.'

One night Sara stayed awake watching over Liam. She knew he was very ill.

'Don't you dare call a doctor,' he whispered. She stroked his pale forehead, feeling a renewal of her care that she had lost while he bullied her. Tenderness replaced terror. A wild longing to rescue him filled her heart. Yet she felt helpless, cut off from all normal society. It was a mild night , a low moon dipped from one side of the small window to the other. As if in answer to her wishes Ruby crept in on her way to bed and sat with her.

Sara stared at her solemnly. 'Is he going to die?'

Ruby's eyes were lustrous in the moonlight. 'No. He'll pull round.'

'I think he wants to die,' said Sara.

Ruby hugged her. 'I've seen it before. He's not strong, he's overdosed but he'll get through. You'll see.I've been like that and I always recover.' They held hands and smiled at each other.

'Let's get some sleep. Dave's downstairs, he's in the same state. Come and sleep in my bed. You can't do any good here, anymore than I can downstairs.' They crept into Ruby's room and lay down with their arms round each other like sisters. The moon was in the window and transformed the room into a pale, delicate place, full of mysterious silver objects.

It was the moon that saved them, thought Sara illogically; it had shone benignly on all of them, the secret circle of friends, the core of her present life. How could she leave them now? They were in it together and would never leave each other, especially now Mum was in Australia. Liam was like a moth near a candle, hovering unceasingly round the glow that drugs cast on his captured life. He could not resist the glow, even when it singed his life.

A few days later he was on his feet again, defiantly ignoring his own weakness. In those few days Sara had come to recognise that she could not rescue him, that without drugs he felt insecure and ill at ease, consumed with the need for more and more stimulants. Was that why he drew near her, saying he needed her? She was his girl.

'But I am your girl.'

'Not really, not until -'

'Not until what?'

He was holding the syringe over her arm. 'Not until I mainline you.'

Why didn't she run away? Wasn't this the ultimate bullying? Or was it the ultimate intimacy. He wanted her to be exactly where he was, he wanted to pull her down into the gutter where she would never dance beneath the stars. She moved away then but he grabbed her and she could do nothing about it because he became loving, gentle, kindly and she wasn't sure how to resist him. Was he trying to make her in his own image so they would go down together? Did she want to go down with him? She had never thought like that before. If only she could get angry with him. If only- but she felt weak and bound and unable to pull herself away.

Chapter thirteen

The living's rough

Dave pushed back his hair. It was long now and curled over his shoulders. He had just come in with more meat he had stolen from another butcher's. He was going to cook it this time. 'We can't go on like this,' he said, 'We need money, that's what we need.' He sat down on the sofa. 'I have an idea. I saw Si the other day. He's looking for somewhere to go, The Fuzz are closing in. What about hiding him here in exchange for whatever he's got? He'll be out of reach of The Fuzz and we'll get the Crack.'

'It might not be like that,' said Liam, 'They might follow him here. I don't want them to find me.'

Dave looked at him hard and swore. 'We let *you* in, didn't we? Si's been a good friend to you as well as me. You've known him forever.'

'You get off my back.'

But it was true, Si had been a good friend to him. There was the dancing night, he told Sara and as he told the story she pictured it with ease.

He and Si, blown out of their minds, danced round the cave in pink slippers, or that's how it seemed. Every object glinted like treasure. Even the curtains were tapestries hanging over the walls, depicting knights in armour in battle with strange animals, half human, half animal, with flowing tails and ferocious eyes. They even stepped out and stood in the room, facing each other but not moving. Si and he danced round them, magically, powerfully, keeping them at bay. In the back of his mind he knew he should be visiting his mum, but hey, she was OK, she was on the mend. He would see her tomorrow. What was wrong with that? They danced on until they crumpled onto the carpet, like fallen angels, and fell into a fevered sleep.

Si turned up in the middle of the night. They were all downstairs sniffing coke. There was a light knock at the door; then they heard it again.

'The Fuzz would knock down the door,' said Dave. He moved cautiously through the dark hall to the front door. There was a chain still dangling from the lock, a reminder of previous respectability.

'Let me in.'

'Oh, it's you!'

Dave slid the chain loose and opened the door. Si slipped in as if he was a huge shadow. He was wearing a dark flowing cloak that hid his flamboyant clothes and merged with the darkness of the hall.

'They're tracking me.'

'You mean they followed you?' Liam looked anxious.

'What you so nervous for? I got a taxi, didn't I, jumped out at the lights, soon disappeared in the crowd. God knows where they are now.'

Ruby came out into the hall. 'Come on upstairs.'

'You better get up there quick as a rabbit,' said Liam, looking round anxiously.

'We'll have a good time,' said Si as he followed Ruby up to the attic.

'It's a small room, more like a large cupboard,' said Ruby, 'but there's a mattress in there. You better stay there until we have the all clear. Can you stand the dark?'

Si whipped out a torch from under his enveloping cloak. 'And I've got something to read,' he said.

'I'll bring you up a hamburger, we have one left over.'

Ruby opened the door and flashed the torch onto debris that must have been there for years and years before the clothes; an old Christmas tree, a carpet sweeper, a bag of old toys.

'Toy cupboard,' she said, 'Look at this old teddy bear.' It was small and brown with beady eyes and a ragged red ribbon tied in a bow round its neck. Si laughed. 'I'll call it JoJo, my mate.' He looked round. 'I don't need to be here all the time. Just for a while now, in case they followed me, and whenever there's that knock at the door. Can I open the door from this side?' He shut himself in and pushed the door open again. 'Bit claustrophobic. Got anything else?'

'It's the best place,' said Ruby.

'Used to space,' said Si. 'Tell you what – I'll stay up here for a bit and only go in there if I need to. Reckon they'll find it anyway. Anything else?'

Liam had followed them up the stairs.

'In our room there's an opening to the roof,' said Sara.

It hadn't been lifted for a long time. Si stood on a chair and pushed his head through. A draft of cold air came down onto the bed and Sara wished she had said nothing. She didn't want this man leaping up there whenever he needed to. Si shut the trapdoor and came down again. 'That's more like it. I can climb all over the roofs. I'll bring the mattress into this room.'

Sara protested but Liam hugged his friend. 'Old times,' he said, as if she didn't count.

'I got plenty,' said Si. 'Let's all stick around up here.' He dragged the mattress from the toy cupboard and put it down next to Liam. 'Now, see what I've got for you.' He laughed as he injected the teddy bear. 'Join in the fun, eh JoJo?'

That night three of them slept in the room, side by side. Sara lay there, wide awake, her mind racing.

It's an intrusion, how dare he come and sleep here. Who does he think he is? Then at some hour when the moon was low in the sky Liam moved over towards Si and curled his arms round him. Sara's heart sank. Yes, Si was an old friend, but what was Liam doing? Where did this leave her?

Was he - ? This was deeper than bullying. It was a silent intrusive rejection. Or had she taken it the wrong way? She didn't think so. She had heard many of his stories about Si and had often wondered where their feelings took them. She was filled with an acute jealousy, it felt like an arrow stuck into her heart. Every time she moved restlessly on the mattress the arrow drove deeper into her body. And yet they weren't doing anything, just cuddling each other as if it was the natural thing to do. Was

Liam feeling protective? It was no good. Her rational thoughts did nothing to remove her suspicion and her only respite was an hour's sleep towards morning.

'I don't want him to sleep with us,' she said, when she and Liam were alone in the kitchen making porridge.

'What you talking about?' said Liam.

'Makes me unhappy, you cuddling him like that.'

'You got a dirty mind, that's what you got.'

She felt unable to reply, and now, because Si had no end of Speed and Crack and Acid tabs she used drugs more than she had ever done before. She felt trapped, no longer by her own betrayal of Liam, but by the tangled feelings that lodged in her heart, as if at last the Minotaur had caught her and there was no way out of the dark cave. Her only consolation was talking to Rubes who listened and understood her despair. On nights when Dave stayed downstairs she crept into Ruby's room and they told each other stories to remind themselves of the other life which seemed so far away. Sometimes Rubes sang to her in her deep, rich voice, quietly, expressing a gentleness that was hard to find in the squat.

Call me up, I'll say I'm fine
be around, I've got the time,
count the cost, tell me the score,
there's no running any more.
Palm to palm we were as one,
without words we'd just begun,
my soul's hungry, my soul is raw,
there's no running any more.

Then Sara would tell her a story, especially ones that were about her Dad.

'When I was knee high to a grass hopper he made me look at the stars. It was winter and Orion was stalking the sky like a great powerful giant. He said I had a Celtic imagination but should remember that the main thing about looking at the stars was to give you perspective.'

Together they leaned out of the small window but only the moon showed up in the pollution of light. Sara was comforted talking about Dad to Ruby and for the moment her anguish faded. Then it returned and she knew that talking to Ruby was no cure, just a moment of comfort.

She became very pale and very thin. Her lethargy, like Liam's, grew day by day.

As time went by, the dusty window of their room became dustier, hazing out the early summer sun. The mattresses got more scruffy, the blankets stank, and with Si in the room Sara lost all incentive to do anything about it.

Si was getting restless. 'Look, Liam, it's good to be with you but don't forget I'm trapped too like you lot. I'll take another week, then I'll risk going out. What do you think?'

'You mean leave us behind?' said Liam in a tone that made Sara shiver. Si smiled. 'This ain't the only place for giving up the gold.'

They fed themselves haphazardly on porridge and bread and milk, then settled in the living room listening to music, injecting. It was always Dave who went out from time to time to steal food and see if anyone was hanging around. Once he was nearly caught and for a week afterwards they lived on porridge and bread. Then he went off again and they waited tensely for him to come back. It gave them a sense of camaraderie, they were all in it together; they didn't need the world and the world didn't need them.

If need be they'd go down together.

Yet somehow, somewhere inside her, Sara kept a little measure of remembrance. She could still faintly hear Dad's voice: *I'll be with you whatever happens.* His voice was ghostly like his image in the park, but it kept her going. She couldn't respond except by telling herself from time to time that one day, despite everything, she would go home.

Then one morning, when Liam was slumped over Si and Dave was downstairs lying flat on the sofa and Pete and Steve were out of it on coke, Ruby said to Sara: 'I have to get out, Sara. I always did suffer from claustrophobia. I'm getting it big now and need to breathe. We don't have to say anything because no-one will follow us. Come on, Sara, let's go up to Hyde Park. Plenty of air there. They'll think we're tourists.'

'We need money.'

Ruby laughed. 'Don't worry, I've got a Big Ben.'

'How much is that?'

'Ten pounds. I stole it from Dave's pocket. I doubt if he'll even remember he had it. Anyhow, it isn't clean money and it's better we spend it quickly.'

They took the underground to Marble Arch, crossed the busy road and as soon as they could, sat down on the grass. 'It's like being out of prison,' said Ruby. 'Why didn't we do it before?'

Sara looked for a long time at Rubes. 'Mindset. We were all in it together. We didn't think we could go.'

They stretched out and closed their eyes. It was a green and yellow day; a hint of summer was in the air. After the damp squat the warm air caressed them and relaxed them. The sun settled on their eyelids in a warm glow. In her mind's eye Sara could see Mum in her late spring garden surrounded by violas and forget-me-nots, tulips, grape hyacinths, the last of the daffodils and the first tiny hint of rosebuds; everything fragrant and well tended. Then she saw the wild roses that flowered in the unkempt estate where they visited every summer, down in Dorset. There was the long, winding drive, lined by laurels and rhododendron bushes. The trees concealed the view, but there was a bend where the bushes and trees ended. There, in the valley, you could see the cottage, secluded and safe, surrounded by pink and white roses in earthenware pots. Beyond were gentle green fields where sheep or cows grazed, backed by hills that gave the further side of the valley a wilder and more mysterious presence.

A sense of great futility came over her. For the first time she could see clearly that her disappearance must have caused great pain.

'I've been thinking of Mum,' she said to Ruby, 'She's not like your Mum at all. Up to now I've had this fantasy that she's gone to Australia with Ben. But Mum isn't really the sort to do that. I've just been so angry with her. I couldn't think straight.' She paused and then said emphatically, 'I am going home, Ruby. I really mean it this time. I don't care about Ben taking Dad's place any more. I want to see everybody and I want them to see me. You see, I think I've caused them a lot of pain.'

'Better not tell Liam.'

'I'm not helping him, Ruby, I'm getting like him.'

'Are you going straight away?'

'I can't, I haven't got money. I haven't got my things.'

Ruby slipped her arm into Sara's. 'I will miss you, you know.'

'Why don't you come home with me?'

Ruby shook her head. 'Can't go back there. My Mum doesn't want me , I know she doesn't. I interfere with her affairs. And if she goes off I can't pay the rent. I'm safer here with Dave. At least I have a roof over my head. Anyhow with all this speed and acid and smack - haven't you thought of that - how you'll miss it?'

'I want you to come with me, Rubes,' Sara pleaded. 'You're the only one who counts.'

There was a silence between them. Now it was Ruby who was remembering those days long ago before she had met Dave, before she had to escape into another world. Maybe it was possible to make sense of life despite all that had happened. She turned her warm gaze on Sara.

'All right then, I'll come,' she said, 'Maybe things will be different.'

'Will you really?'

They sat up and put their palms against each other as they had when they were children. Then they got up and walked on, hand in hand; for the first time, together, they felt the possibility of a new life. This hope made everything look different: the greenness of the grass was a revelation, as if they had never seen grass before. All around them children were running and laughing and shouting, as they used to do when they were small. The trees were full of birds whistling and flying round, dogs were wagging their tails and sniffing the grass, the sun bathed them as if they had never felt its warmth before. For a short moment what was normal seemed to be a paradise of freedom. So when they sat on a bench and Ruby found she was sitting on someone's mobile phone it seemed part and parcel of their magical experience.

She fiddled with the phone and it lit up. 'Hey, Sara, why don't you try again? They might be there. Come on, I'll do it for you.' She pressed the numbers out and handed the mobile to Sara.

It was Emily's voice, clear and familiar. 'I can't hear. Who is it, please?'

Sara's voice stuck like a lump in her throat.

'I can't hear.'

Sara spoke like a shadow. 'Emily, it's me.'

There was a long pause.

'Sara, where are you? We've been looking everywhere. Mum had to give up work because Ben went off to be with his son in Australia and she's been looking for you all the time. Please don't go. Where are you? Please answer.'

Suddenly, Sara's voice cleared. 'I'm coming home, Emily. Tell Mum I'm coming home.'

Emily's voice came in a rush. 'You weren't on the downs, were you? I looked up there. I thought you were up there with our white horse. But you weren't.'

'Tell Mum I'm all right.'

'Why have you been away for so long?'

Sara's voice closed up again.

'Are you still there? Sara, are you there?'

'I'm coming home,' Sara said hoarsely. 'Rubes and me are coming home.'

Part three

There's no running
any more

Chapter fourteen

Going there and back again

When they went back for their things they found the front door of the squat had been kicked down. It hung on its hinges, lopsided, the inside chain dangling,

'Hey, what's happened? What have they been doing? Is Dave all right?' Ruby voiced their fear and instantly, almost like a habit, they were back in the other world, feeling the pull of concern, unable to shake off their connection. They squeezed past the hanging door and into the hall. They were immediately struck by the silence.

'What's happened? Where have they gone?'

They ran through the house quietly. Were the intruders waiting to leap out at them? Ruby's room was trashed; had they booted the mattress to one side because someone was hiding under it? In Sara's room the trap door to the roof was shut, but from the position of the chair Si and Liam had either tried or succeeded in escaping through it. In a whirlwind of fear that broke and banished their thoughts in the park, they clung together, collapsing on the floor , wondering if the others had all been caught or if they had given The Fuzz the slip. They felt helpless, overwhelmed. It was Sara who recovered first. She pulled Ruby up, held her tight and whispered.

'We have to go. The Fuzz will be back sooner or later. We can't do any good hanging around.'

Any small object they possessed had been taken or trashed so they ran downstairs empty-handed silent, wondering if they would crash into The Fuzz and be taken down. They could scarcely breathe as they stepped through the broken door and out into the darkening road. Were they being watched? Was that man lighting up over there hanging around to trap them? Was this woman coming towards them one of them in disguise?

'Let's go back inside,' said Ruby, her glistening brown eyes wide with fear. 'Come on, let's go back, it's safer in there.'

She pulled Sara round to the back of the house and through the broken door. This time they were more aware of the damage. In the kitchen the bread and porridge from the larder was shoved onto the kitchen table, and the table itself was pushed up against the wall. On the stove, the burnt saucepan was on its side and a trickle of porridge ran down onto the floor. In the room where they spent most of their time the cushions of the old sofa were split open, lying in a heap on the floor, limp and disembowelled. Magazines and mugs were scattered and broken, the thin red curtains were half pulled down. The decaying pelmet hung on one hook. Had there been a fight? They raced upstairs again and into Sara's room. The mattresses had been split open, the fire grate disturbed, the cigarette stubs raked through, Sara's cheap pink soap thrown into the middle of the sink. There was nothing left except a heap of torn or broken objects, piled up under the window. JoJo was lying flat on his back, his stomach ripped open. Poor JoJo. Liam's haversack, that he took everywhere with him, was missing. No message, nothing.

They scarcely knew what they were doing. They sat down on one of the torn mattresses and looked up . There was a sparrows' nest in the roof and they could hear the birds twittering up there. They sat in a trance of fear as if they were two of those baby birds who had fallen out of that nest and couldn't get back.

It was then they heard a creaking sound, a scratching. Open-mouthed and holding each other fearfully, they watched the trap door in the ceiling slowly open. A pair of long thin legs in jeans dangled down and found a footing on the chair.

'Liam! Liam!'

Liam sat down on the floor to recover his breath. 'They never got me,' he boasted. 'Got the others but not me.' He didn't ask about them, simply looked round. Their relief was so great they started to laugh hysterically. Fancy Liam landing on them like a dark angel from the sky! He grew impatient and talked urgently.

'I came back to get you. Had a hunch you'd be around. Now listen to me. We can't stay here no more. Not for a few days. We

114

can come back when things have calmed down.'

He held Sara's hands and pleaded with her to go with him. He needed her more than ever, she couldn't leave now, and besides, they would soon go home together. Emily's voice became a wafer-thin wail in Sara's mind. Of course they would go home together, isn't that what he said? But not now, it was too dangerous now. He was in real danger, they were all in real danger.

She could no longer work things out logically.

'Where are you thinking of going?' said Ruby, disentangling herself from Sara and standing up. Her voice was distrustful; she was shaking her head at Sara as if to say, *Can't you see he's not stable? He's tagged you along all the time, you might as well be a dog with a collar and lead.*

Liam took charge. 'No need to get like that. We'll lie low for two or three days. Things pass, it shouldn't be for long.'

Sara stood up and pulled Ruby's arm. 'He's right, Rubes, we do have to go, all of us. We don' t want to get caught as well, do we?'

'Dave, I want to know about Dave,' said Ruby, unwilling to move until she knew. 'What happened to him, where is he?'

'I don't know,' said Liam impatiently, 'I was up here, he was downstairs with the others.'

'You know more than that,' said Ruby, 'How am I going to get hold of him again?'

Liam's temper was rising. 'We have to get going.'

'And I have to know '

'Come on, Rubes,' said Sara, 'He'll tell you as we go along.'

'I want to know what's happened to Dave,' screamed Ruby.

'Stop going on, you bitch. I'll tell you what happened when we're on the move. We'll all get caught if we stay here. The Fuzz said they'll be back and they will be.'

Liam pushed the girls downstairs and towards the back door. 'Come on, get a move on now.'

Sara held Ruby's hand. She saw the look of despair in her friend's eyes and wanted to comfort her. But there was no time, no reason to stay longer. Now Liam was here he would know where to go, he would know where to take them. She didn't allow herself to think otherwise. The world had turned upside down again and it seemed there was nothing else to do but follow him. In a way it was a relief to let events take hold of her again.

Outside was less fearful now Liam was with them. 'Where are we going?' Sara asked, looking up and down the road. Liam turned to the right and they followed him without question. 'I know another place,' he said, 'up this way.' He looked at Ruby, 'Dave told me.'

Darkness was falling and a light rain shone in the light from shops and houses like swarms of tiny insects. There was a noise ahead of them, people shouting and arguing, the interfering voice of the law. Liam turned and ran back.

'You don't know what you're doing,' shouted Ruby.

'We're not going to get caught by that lot, or do you want to? We'll go up the Dilly, sure to meet someone up there with a place. You always do.'

Sara stopped dead. Was Ruby right? Was Liam making everything up as he went along? Unsummoned, a picture of Emily filled her mind. Her sister was on the downs, running towards the white horse, arms outstretched, waiting to meet her.

'Don't stop now,' said Liam, impatiently. 'We've got to get away. You keep right next to me.'

They followed him because they no longer knew what to do. They held hands, knowing in their hearts Liam had no idea either. Going somewhere seemed better than staying still, that was all. I'll phone again soon, thought Sara, at least they know I'm all right.

She smiled at Ruby as they raced along, trying to avoid disaster. Ruby smiled back, a querying smile, almost as if she had given up. Now, for a moment Sara felt stronger than Ruby.

Liam was half running down the road and they had difficulty keeping up with him.

'They never could catch me, the bastards,' he said, hurrying them along, mocking and swearing and laughing. He rushed them into the Underground where they pooled the little amount of money they had between them and bought tickets.

'So what happened?' said Rubes persistently, as they stood swaying in the crowded train.

'OK then.'

Everything was peaceful, he told them, even Si decided to go downstairs. It was one of those moments in the squat when they felt settled. They were all banging up and telling each other stories about the past. He and Si were remembering those early days when it seemed no-one and nothing could touch their way of carrying on. They were laughing together, reliving those moments. For once there was a sort of normality in the squat.

Sara felt a pang of jealousy; they seemed so close together.

'Then there was this noise outside,' said Liam. 'Well, we didn't take too much notice at first. We were way back, see, talking about when we were small. That's why Si said he wanted Jo Jo to join in and I said I'd go and get him. We were in that sort of mood, see? Well, the truth is, if I hadn't gone upstairs on that daft mission to fetch Jo Jo for Si, I'd have been caught as well.'

Sara and Ruby were leaning towards him, trying to catch every word between the noise of the train and people shuffling and talking. Liam looked at Ruby and shrugged. 'When I heard the shouting and fighting I made for the roof. I was meant to go on, wasn't I?'

'And what about Dave?' whispered Ruby angrily, 'You didn't think of going to help him then?'

'How could I have helped him? I'd have got caught as well.'

The train doors opened and they peered out. No, they hadn't gone far enough yet.

Liam went on: 'I was on the roof , wasn't I, lying behind the chimney. I didn't dare lift my head to see what was going on down in the road. I couldn't believe my luck. They'd trashed everything looking for gear, but they'd missed the trap door in the roof! If they'd noticed it they'd have come up and got me.'

He was up there for a good two hours, he told them. That was it. They knew the rest. Sara looked at Ruby. 'We were lucky too,' she said, 'and don't you worry about Dave. He'll be all right.'

'We're none of us all right,' said Ruby. 'How are we going to make out for the next few days?'

They spoke softly together, relying on the indifference of the passengers.

'We'll go home soon,' said Sara.

'Not yet,' said Liam quickly, grabbing Sara's hand. ' We must stay together. Until things have calmed down. I've got a good idea. You can sing, Rubes. You've got the voice of an angel. You could make a lot of money singing in the subway. We can hide in the crowd while you do it.'

'Thanks' said Ruby coldly. 'What about you, what will you do?'

Sara took her arm. 'I know how you feel, Rubes. I know how much you're missing Dave. But we're all in the same boat, we're all getting hungry and we've nothing much, have we? No dope. Nothing.'

Liam winked. 'Don't you be so sure! Si gave me everything I wanted that evening, everything he could.' He swung round to Ruby. 'What about singing for a meal or two in exchange?'

'Anything to dull the pain,' said Ruby.

As they got out of the train at Bank they stopped at the end of the platform and lit up, 'Nothing like crack to soothe the system,' said Liam. 'Now we'll make for Tottenham Court Road. Lots of people go through the subway and like a bit of cheering up.'

The idea took hold of them, so they made for the Central Line and boarded a train for Tottenham Court Road.

That evening no-one else was busking in the subway so Liam carefully chose a position halfway to one of exits. 'Sara and me will stay around,' he said to Rubes, 'We'll listen for the clink of coins.'

They hung back, and after a while Ruby twisted up her scarf and placed it on the ground, ready to receive her reward. She began to sing their song in her rich, dark, easy voice:

Where is love if it's rented out,
where is hope if it's full of doubt.
Freedom's more than an open door,
there's no running any more.

But I'll be running through the wind and rain,
going there and back again.
Don't go asking where I'll roam,
''cos I've got no home.
Because I've got no home.

Sara listened entranced, she was filled with a sort of hope.
Maybe Ruby's singing might be their way out; she didn't know
how or why, but it was possible, she thought. She had never
been so aware of Ruby's voice as she was at that moment. She
forgot the subway was draughty and cold and that people came
down the steps as if they were sucked by some invisible vacuum,
hair blowing in the draught, coats billowing out. Perhaps it was
the crack that made her feel like this, or standing beside Liam
who might well have copped it with the others. But, no, you
had to give it to Rubes, her voice so richly filled the subway, it
subverted the low lights and grey shadows and hurrying people
into a kingdom of sunshine and song. Another strange thing
happened. Unexpectedly behind Rubes's singing Sara could hear
Dad's voice, a long way off but somehow near her: *'Don't be sad,*
darling, I'll always love you wherever you are.'
Even here? thought Sara. Yes, she believed even here Dad
was loving her, in some strange, far distant way, looking after her.
Ruby's scarf was gradually filling up with coins as the people
felt lifted up by her voice. Someone had even dropped a small
message on lined paper that settled among the coins like a small
paper boat. Soon there was enough to get a small meal.
They found a little café where Ruby bought them all bowls
of homemade onion soup and chunks of fresh bread and mugs
of hot, steaming tea. Sara spooned the soup ravenously into her
mouth.
'Thanks, Rubes, I knew you could do it. You ought to do
something with that voice of yours.'
'Never heard you sing so well before,' said Liam.
'She's always sung.' Sara smiled at Ruby. 'Do you remember
when you used to sing in the choir at school?' They laughed at
the thought.

'You in a school choir?' said Liam, 'Never!'

'Oh yes.' Ruby cupped her chin and looked into the distance. 'Come along, girls, all together, mouths open wide. One, two, three - Hark the Herald Angels sing.....'

Liam interrupted. 'The law's come in. Over there. Don't turn round. Take no notice.' Sara felt the freedom and Emily and hope fall away. She slumped down in her plastic chair, overcome by a great weariness. She warmed her hands round the mug and looked at Liam who was holding himself slightly stiffly, as if this would make him invisible. Ruby was bristling with a terror that shone in her dark eyes. Sara's heart thudded as one of The Fuzz leaned over her.

'Name, miss?'

'Jennifer Hargreaves and she's my partner,' said Liam in a rush.

'Let her answer for herself.' The policeman looked hard at Sara. 'That's right,' she said hoarsely. The thought made her feel trapped, but she must have sounded convincing because The Fuzz turned to Ruby who came up with ' Jasmine. Jasmine Subeto.' He looked hard at her, then, as if he changed his mind, went over to another couple.

'Now, that's what I call harassment,' said Liam, in a voice not quite loud enough for the policeman to hear. 'You've only got to have a cup of tea and they're after you.'

Ruby and Sara began to giggle and call each other by their pretend names. They put on posh voices and spoke rather loudly. The waiters were looking apprehensive, but nothing came of the incident, and when the policeman had gone they moved about as if nothing had happened. Maybe they were used to it.

Sara was still thirsty. 'Have we enough for another mug?'

'If we share one.' So they ordered another tea and passed it round the table.

Ruby put her arm round Sara. - 'Fancy thinking The Fuzz were after us.' They laughed, but in the back of her mind Sara felt a foreboding that she couldn't shake off.

They went outside. Rain was spiking off the pavement and

the wind cut like a cold blade down the street. 'Where are we going to sleep?' asked Sara, as they huddled together.

'There are places,' said Ruby. 'I think there's one in Shaftsbury Avenue. That's if we don't find somewhere else.' The two girls looked at Liam and he tightened his arms round both of them. Dimly, Sara understood how he was feeding on the situation, but she was too confused to bring her thoughts into focus.

He was looking down at them with an air of authority. 'The Fuzz might get us there. Don't worry, I'll find us somewhere.' With crude self-confidence he led the girls through the streets. Lights and buildings blurred in the rain. They walked through pools of darkness in streets where there were no shops, only rows of tall, dark buildings.

Sara pulled away. 'I'm not going any further. I'm too tired.'

'Here,' said Liam, shoving his hands deeply into his pocket, 'I told you to lean on Uncle Liam. Help all round.' He brought out his little silver dragon tin, opened it slowly and handed round little wraps of speed as if they were sweets. After this they gave up worrying.

Chapter fifteen

Full of doubt

That night to appease Liam they slept with the tramps and the homeless on the embankment near Charing Cross. No-one was meant to doss down here but where could they go? There were never enough places for everyone. If they hadn't been high they would have choked at the smell and sight of old, crumpled bodies, thrown like broken gargoyles carelessly to the ground.

Sara dreamed that Ruby was singing to her. They were in a buttercup field sitting under a huge old oak tree. The song was so sweet Sara wanted to do nothing but listen to it, and she knew Rubes was so happy she wanted to do nothing but sing. A little way off Emily was picking buttercups; Mum and Dad were walking round the field arm in arm. Birds were singing too, hidden by the leaves of the oak tree that made a lace pattern on the grass. She felt secure, surrounded by all the people she loved. When she woke she lay with her eyes shut, savouring her dream.

Liam wasn't in it, and that mattered; she had the feeling that if he had been in her dreams she would have had to stay with him forever. She would give him one more day, she decided; then she and Ruby would be off.

She drifted back to sleep and this time there was a voice in her head reading to her from a book. It was a deep, formal voice that had authority, not one she knew. Yet it reminded her of the time her father told her stories. Perhaps it was his ghost voice.

You are on a circuit, Sara. It will take you from squat to squat, drug scene to drug scene; it will give you a fellow feeling with others who are travelling the same way, a sense of belonging, a warmth that protects you from an alien world. At first, the circuit seems broad and easy. Haven't the famous walked along it - the poets, the music makers, the rebels, the revolutionaries - the people whose lives are in the story books? The track is well worn and brings many people to the same place where drugs may become the only reason for living, the only reason for dying. Soon that broad and easy path becomes a little, grey, magnetic pinpoint. The force you need to lift away from it is so great it can only be given by the hands of someone outside, or by the silent hands of Death, who frees us all.

Normally a voice in her head would have frightened her. But this voice was welcome, telling her what she knew already but could hardly admit. Then she remembered her father saying, *'Don't be sad, darling, I'll always love you wherever you are.'* and she knew for sure the two voices were connected.

When she woke up in the night Ruby was fidgeting from side to side, rubbing her hips, wiggling her toes.

'What's the matter?'

'Are you joking?' Ruby's brown eyes gleamed in the lamplight. 'This is the last time I'm going to camp out.' She sat up. Liam was between them, groaning in his sleep. 'I'm aching all over. Old before my time.' She looked angrily at Liam. 'You know what he's doing, don't you, Sara?'

'I had this dream and in a funny way it told me.' She stretched over Liam and rubbed Ruby's back, up and down, trying to ease the ache. She looked down at Liam's thin , crumpled body. 'He's stringing us along with his crack and speed. Thinks that will keep us with him. I never really thought like that before, Rubes.' She looked round at the men and women in cardboard boxes and ragged sleeping bags. A dog was curled up; his bones showed in the lamplight.

'We don't have to be here,' said Ruby, wriggling her shoulders. 'I'm sure there's places where we can go - like the Sally Army.'

Sara rubbed her hands together and massaged Ruby's legs. 'There are. I'm sure there are. The thing is, Liam doesn't want to be seen, that's what it is, so he's dragged us along with him to this hell hole. It's funny, Rubes, for the first time for ages and ages, I don't feel it's disloyal to leave him. He's pulling me down, he's pulling you down too. I've always known it but it's been muddled up with me betraying him. I never thought of what he was doing to me. Same with Dave, isn't it?'

Ruby hesitated. 'I don't know.'

'Yes, you do,'

'What's got into you, Sara? You sound grown-up. Don't know if I like it. Love and loyalty, that's what I like in you.'

Sara looked worried. 'I'm still the same me. It's just that I had these two dreams. Well, they were not like dreams really, more like warnings.'

'That's crack for you.'

Sara stood up and moved round to Ruby. She cuddled up to her. 'No, it was something different. Tell you what, I first began to feel different when you sang in that subway.'

'What's my singing got to do with it?'

'Oh, Rubes, you mustn't waste your singing.'

'Never heard you talk like this before.'

'I told you, I feel different. I can't explain it except to say it's like I see things straight. What on earth are we doing here, Rubes?'

'Captured,' said Ruby, and Sara moved over to sit with her. Their arms entwined round each other they told a story, one following on the other as they used to when they were at school, in little girl voices, whispering as they did ages ago at the back of the classroom.

'Once upon a time there was a spider looking for flies,' began Rubes.

'It was not a normal spider,' went on Sara, 'It was huge with big green eyes and a black body and legs that were long and thin and powerful. Its web hung from the branch of a chestnut tree and it spent all its life catching flies.'

Ruby was about to take up the story when Liam groaned loudly and shook. He put out his hand and panicked when he couldn't feel Sara. 'I'm ill.'

'You're not the only one,' said Ruby, 'We're all ill. We're all flies in the web, aren't we, Sara?'

'I can't move. I need a fix.' He lifted his head and found Sara on the other side of him. 'I need a fix.'

Sara spoke gently. ' Liam, try and go to sleep.'

125

'I need a fix,' he repeated pathetically.

'All that talk,' said Ruby as Sara fumbled in his rucksack, found the syringe and gave it to Liam. 'I could do with that, I could do with being out of it altogether.'

Sara went back to her friend and put her arms round her. 'Come on, Rubes, we'll get you cured, that's what we'll do.'

'You must be joking, who's going to cure me?'

Ruby went through her pockets. 'Nothing. I've got nothing. Get that tin of his over here. I can't stand it, honestly I can't.' She went through her pockets again. 'This is all I've got.' It was a folded up piece of paper.

'What's that?'

'It was in the scarf when I was getting the money.'

Sara snatched it and opened it. She screwed up her eyes in the lamplight. 'Listen to this, Rubes,' but Ruby was already reaching out for the tin and stuffing her face.

Sara read the note, *'You should do more with a voice like yours.'* She looked up. 'Then there's a telephone number,' but Ruby was no longer listening to her. She had the tin in her hands and was offering it to Sara.

Thoughts ran through Sara's mind so fast she could hardly keep up with them. What was this note doing in her hand if it wasn't to let her know there was a way out, not just for her but for Rubes as well. It wasn't Liam' way out. His was the long hiding away from reality, the dumbing down, the escape into dreams. It was a harder way and it depended on a decision.

'No thanks, Rubes, I'm fine.'

It wasn't quite as simple as that. She looked at the tin, lying in the circle of Ruby's hands. She was tempted, but she could still hear the dream voice in her head and had the feeling it was now or never.

'Be like that,' said Ruby and closed the tin. Sara snatched it back and opened it. There wasn't all that much left. Speed, smack, special K, crack, all that Si had off-loaded on Liam had mostly gone. A few acid tabs and doves were left. She picked up an ecstasy pill and then with difficulty put it down again. The voice was still telling her what to do.

She lay down in between Ruby and Liam. They were both drifting off again. She felt stiff and cold and sat up and pulled her anorak round her shoulders more tightly, trying to keep out the cold air. The grey light lay on the bodies near her, on their creased, dirty clothes, their faces hidden by hoods or knitted hats pulled over their ears and eyes. Darkness settled on strips of tarmac that lay between them, they were like fallen sculptures. *Is this how I want to be?* Sara turned to look at Ruby, then she lay down again and dozed fitfully. In her dreams the tramps were fixed by nails onto a cardboard cathedral. Rain softened the cardboard and poured like white milk out of the mouths of the gargoyles. She reached up and let the silky white liquid pour into her mouth. When she woke up she had a strong desire for milk.

She ached with damp and cold. She stood up and was appalled at the pain in her legs and arms. She walked with difficulty over to the newsagents . It was a small stall that might sell milk.

'I need some milk,' she told the old man. His crinkly blue eyes looked her up and down.

'You look as if you need a bit more than that.'

Sara nodded. 'Could I have some milk?'

'I'm not running a charity,' said the man but he must have been touched by her thin pale face and maybe by the straightforward way in which she spoke.

'Why don't you get home?' he said.

'I'm going to. I've been sleeping out here with friends.'

'The sooner you get home the better, my dear. Here -'

He handed her a carton of milk and she took it gratefully. Her heart warmed. 'How can I thank you enough?'

'By getting back home.'

She swigged down some of the milk. 'I'll keep this for my friend.'

The newsagent nodded. They were strangers, thought Sara, but in that short while the man's kindness bridged the distance between them. It didn't seem difficult to say, 'Where can I have a wash?'

He laughed. 'At least you don't go dirty. Tell you what, you should find somewhere in Charing Cross. Stations always have loos. Here, take this.'

He held out a five pound note. Tears filled her eyes. 'Why are you doing this for me?'

He pursed his lips and rubbed his hands together nervously. 'You remind me of my daughter,' he said.

'What happened to her?'

'You're a curious one.' He paused, as if even thinking about her was painful. 'She got in with a bad lot at school. About your age. Died of an overdose.'

'I'm sorry, I'm really sorry.'

'Them drugs, they're a scourge on the land. Now you get home fast as you can, do you hear me?' He spoke urgently as if it was his daughter who was in front of him.

'What was her name?'

'Lucy. She looked like you.'

'I'll get home,' she told him, as if he was her father.

Ruby was stirring painfully. 'Last time I'm going to do this.'

'Here, have some.'

Ruby sat up painfully and rubbed her legs. She yawned widely. 'Hell – that's what I call this.'

Sara gave her the remains of the milk. 'I've got some money. That really nice newsagent gave it to me.'

'What does he want then?'

'He doesn't. He said I was like his daughter. He lost her, you see. She died of an overdose. He wants us to get home.'

'What about him?'

All this time Liam had not moved. Sara shook him and he half woke. 'Think I've got jaundice.'

Ruby and Sara looked at each other. 'We'll have to get a doctor,' said Ruby. 'I think he's very bad. We'll have to do that first.'

'You're not to call a doctor,' said Liam in a slurred voice. Silence. Sara and Ruby signed to each other. 'They all need doctors,' said Sara, looking round. It was difficult to see if they were men or women, these bundled forms that stirred in the morning light.

With an effort Liam sat up, leaning on one elbow. 'Shut up. I feel weak. Get me the tin.'

Sara didn't move.

'Then I'll get it myself.'

' We're going over to the loos.'

'Are you splitting?'

'Of course we're not,' said Sara.

'He's blackmailing you again,' said Ruby as they walked painfully up the road and into Charing Cross station. 'You can't move without him wanting to control you. He wants you down there where he is.'

Sara got change from the lady in charge of the toilets. They went inside and plunged their hands into hot water. Sara felt so blissful she shut her eyes at the sensation of warmth and softness. She would never ever forget it. All the hardship she had endured was overwhelmed by this moment of pure physical rapture. She knew what thousands and thousands of people in the world must feel when the rains came after a drought.

She looked at Ruby who was splashing her face and laughing. Despite the painful night Ruby looked surprisingly neat. Her curly black hair was uncrushed, her tight bleached jeans only slightly creased. Sara looked at her in admiration. 'How do you do it, Rubes?'

'Practice,' said Ruby. 'Here, borrow my comb, a girl should never travel without one.'

Sara looked at her own wet face in the mirror. It was dark and pale and dim, her eyes were bright and underlined with dark patches, her long coloured hair was matted. She took the comb and worked at the knots, all the time staring at her image in the mirror. She thought she would look different now she felt different, but the face in front of her had trapped the homeless Sara and silently hidden her new spirit.

'But she's there,' she thought, 'and I'm quitting this scene. I'm quitting.'

She looked at Rubes's reflection in the mirror and said again, 'How on earth do you do it? No-one would know.'

'I know,' said Ruby, turning full face to Sara, 'but I'm making damn sure the world doesn't know.'

Sara smiled. 'We'll go and phone,' she said, handing back the comb.

Chapter sixteen

There's no running any more

Sara felt in the pocket of her jacket. 'Enough for a short call, then a coffee.'

'Sounds good,' said Ruby. 'Tell you what, I'll go back while you get on to the dog and bone. Liam might want a coffee too. O.K?'

Sara smiled. 'I don't remember that one!'

It was seven-o-clock and the station was already crowded. The loudspeaker was calling out clear, calm information, the sandwich and coffee bars were open, a group of railway workers were joking loudly together, people were anxiously scanning the information screens, others were pouring in through the ticket barriers.

Sara's heart beat loudly as she dialled home.

'Sara, thank God!' Mum's voice was the sound of a childhood that seemed a long, long, way away. Sara wanted to reply but her own voice wouldn't come. It was halted in some deep chamber of feeling she could barely touch.

'Please, please speak again. Where are you, darling?'

Sara looked up at all the people. For a moment she couldn't remember why she was here. At last, with difficulty, her voice came back. 'We want you to meet us, Mum. Me and Rubes and Liam.'

'I've been waiting such a long time. Oh Sara, please don't go away again.'

Sara said nothing for a while.

'Are you still there?'

Sara nodded and her voice came again, as if it was someone else's. 'We'll be at Waterloo this evening. Nine o'clock.' That would give them plenty of time.

'Whereabouts?'

'There's a red letter box opposite platform one. There's a round booth of phones there too. You can't miss it.'

'I'll see you by the letterbox, darling.'

'Yes.' The receiver felt slippery in her hand. 'Do you know where I mean, Mum?'

'Yes, I know where you mean.'

Sara paused. 'Liam's ill, we're going to sort him out first. You won't tell anyone about him, will you? He trusts you.'

Mum's voice was instant, hasty, reassuring. 'Of course I won't tell anyone. As long as you and Ruby are there. How are you, Sara? Tell me, darling. Are you well?'

She wanted to curl up in Mum's arms. Her head drooped down and she noticed the sole of her canvas shoe flapping where the canvas was torn.

'I need new shoes.'

'Of course you can have new shoes. There's nothing to worry about, Sara. Please don't be frightened. Please, please be there.'

'How's Emily?'

The pips went and Mum's voice spoke behind them, until the click drowned it.

Sara dug in her pocket again and pulled out the screwed up note that she had taken from Ruby. Would it do any good if she phoned it? She went through her money again and there wasn't much left. She put the note back into her pocket. That would be for another time.

She caught sight of Ruby rushing towards her through the crowd. She was waving her hands, as if she was relieved to see Sara.

'How is he?'

'Asleep, stoned, I don't know what. The tin was beside him empty. There was an awful lot in it, Sara. I know, I saw it before. He's too heavy for us to move so we'll have to call someone. We better get an ambulance.'

Sara shook her head. 'Look, Rubes, he said we shouldn't. He might come round, then we can take him home with us. That would be much better for him, wouldn't it?'

'I suppose so. I just didn't like the look of him.'

Sara ran her fingers through her ragged hair. 'Pity we haven't got Dave here.'

Ruby turned on her sharply. 'Don't talk to me of Dave. You know I think about him all the time. If only I knew where he was. '

Sara put her arms round Ruby and tried to soothe her but Ruby was tense and began to sob. It was the first time she had shown her grief.

'Say he's checkin' out. I don't know, do I?'

'Say Liam is checkin' out.'

They looked at each other, horrified at their thoughts.

'No-one's dying,' said Sara firmly, 'No-one. We'll take Liam home with us and then we'll find Dave - watch out, The Fuzz's over there.'

'It doesn't matter now,' said Ruby, 'Come on, let's go and have a coffee. I'll feel better with something inside me. I wish that Liam of yours hadn't taken all the acid tabs. I really need them now.'

They walked over to the coffee stall and Sara bought one carton of black coffee that she handed to Ruby. 'You need it more than me. When you've finished we'll go and sort out Liam.'

His face was old and fragile, but his hands that were spread out over his crumpled parka were slender and young. He stirred as if he sensed she was there. He talked under his breath and Sara bent over him to catch what he was whispering.

'I remember that day, it will never come again, none of it will ever come again. I'd like to get back to our shed on the downs, I liked it there, away from everyone. I didn't mean to get like this, I didn't mean, I wanted...' And in a sharper voice, *'Sara, don't leave me and don't take me to hospital. Don't do nothing.'*

Sara shook her head. ' I promise. Don't you worry any more.'

'It was my best day, they told me I'd pass the exams, they told me I'd get on, they didn't tell me I'd do none of it, they didn't tell me my mum would be ill. It's my best friend Si who's killing me.'

'See what I mean?' whispered Ruby. 'Come on Sara, we'll have to ca`l an ambulance.'

133

Sara held Liam's right hand and put it up to her cheek. 'He doesn't want one.'

"What he thinks is neither here nor there.'

Sara whispered fiercely, 'Yes, it is. Everything went wrong from the moment I told on him. I won't do it again.'

Ruby pulled her hand away and held it tightly. 'This is different, Sara, he's really ill. We haven't got much choice.'

'We'll stay around,' said Sara. 'If he doesn't come round by this evening we'll call the ambulance. It's about freedom,' she said after a while.

'It's about guilt,' said Ruby, 'You shouldn't listen to it. It's a false voice. Anyway I thought you'd got out of it, I thought you were different.'

'Deep inside I am,' said Sara but she wondered if she was. Had that been a passing moment when she had felt free of it all? She looked down at Liam. No, it wasn't that she wanted to stay with him, but you don't kick a friend when they're down, do you? Or was Rubes right – his health had to come first? Liam stirred and smiled at her. It was a weak, distant smile.

'We'll give it a bit longer,' she said .

'We can't stay here for long,' said Ruby, 'We'll get moved on. Tell you what, you haven't had a coffee yet and I could do with another one.' She smiled at Sara who was still looking confused. 'We've got to sort it, that's for sure. Don't you see, if we don't they will.'

'Big sister.'

Ruby opened up Liam's haversack. 'Maybe I'll find some more acid tabs. You never know.'

'So that's what you're after!'

'Hey, look at this!'

She pulled out a ten pound note from one of the pockets.

'He said he didn't have anything,' said Sara, staring at the note unbelievingly.

'Perhaps he'd forgotten himself. Perhaps he stole it. And look, a couple of acid tabs.'

Liam looked as if he was sleeping calmly so they stood up. Ruby stuffed the note and the acid tabs into her pocket.

'The root of all good,' she said, 'Now we can have a bun with our coffee.'

They found a little café up the road. There were plenty of tables and they sat by the window opposite each other. The buns were spicy and sticky and the coffee made them feel warm and comfortable. They ordered another round and Sara pocketed the meagre change they had from the ten pound note.

'I wish we could stay here all day,' said Ruby as they sipped their second lot of coffee slowly. They began telling each other stories as they used to when they were small. Once Upon A Time was still a safe haven. They spoke a few sentences and then the other one took up the plot. Where did this fairy child come from with her fairy godmother and three wishes that no-one must hear? And who was this strange fat man who kept poking his head into the story as if he had a right to be there, next to the fairy queen? Why was he trying to snatch away her wishes with his tiny potent hand-held vacuum cleaner that sucked up everything around it, visible and invisible? They laughed as the story creaked on and on, and when they were bored they toyed with the future by tearing up their paper napkins and pretending they were tarot cards. Ruby looked at Sara dreamily. 'I see someone in well lit attic, waving a paint brush in front of a canvas. She's wearing a filthy old shirt, spattered with paint and there's a faint smile on her face.' She looked up at Sara. 'That's what you're going to be. An artist. At least that's what you used to want to be. I still have the drawing you did of me.'

'That daft thing. Where is it?'

'In my one and only drawer at home.'

'Artist sounds too grand. I used to like drawing but you have to study for that and I'm not going back to school.'

'There's other places where you can hang out.'

'I suppose so, but you have to find the right one. Look what they thought of my drawing at school.'

'That's because you did nothing else.'

'That was before Dad died. After that I did nothing – do you remember how I did nothing? When I gave up drawing Mum was quite pleased. She always said it wouldn't bring in the pennies. Besides the school wasn't too keen. Let's be honest, they wouldn't have me back, not now, and I wouldn't want to go back.'

Sara sipped her coffee and peered at Ruby over the rim. 'I'll go to college or something. What about you?'

'Me? You must be joking. It's all cloud cuckoo land for me. I haven't any money or any qualifications.'

'Nor have I. But we could get them. You can do it at any age. We could go to college together.'

They went on dreaming about the future. covering up their dereliction, their need for drugs, their sense of confusion and most of all the fear of what was happening to Liam and Dave. But eventually they stopped talking and screwed up their torn pieces of napkin and shoved them in their pockets. Ruby took out the acid tabs from her pocket. 'They'll get me through,' she said, 'When this is all over I'll have a go at giving up. Promise you.'

'Let's hope so,' said Sara.

They saw the truth in each other's eyes and knew that grief was never far away and mostly it was hard to bear. For a while they sat in the sort of silence that friends share, then Sara said out of the blue: 'One day at a time, Rubes, that's how we've got to do it. We have to build up, bit by bit. '

Ruby laughed, 'You sound like your grandma.'

'Perhaps I do. I just-' she hesitated, then spoke anxiously, 'I don't want you to go down like Liam and Dave.'

'You must be joking, we couldn't be much more down than we are.'

'I want you to stay with me, that's what I want.'

Ruby nodded. 'Yes, Miss.'

Sara looked at the few tired looking dregs of coffee at the bottom of her mug, flung back her head and drank them up.

'I'd like another coffee and cake,' said Ruby. 'Have we enough?'

'Not quite,' said Sara and went up to the counter and ordered two small scones and some tap water. That would have to do. They pretended the water was vodka and quickly slid into another game to keep themselves from thinking what they might find when they went back to Liam. Sara put down her glass. 'Let's play the future again. We haven't done you yet. I know what you want to be.' Ruby looked blank.

'A singer,' said Sara triumphantly.

'I sing now, don't I?'

'I mean properly.'

'Come off it, Sara, you need money and influence in this world.'

Sara wouldn't let go of the idea. It was as if she was weaving some sort of thread that shone with great possibilities and at the same time took her back to Mum and Emily and Gran, the source, she felt, of all normality. In her mind's eye a picture of her family appeared, delicate and fragile as if it could break at any moment, but radiant, like a picture Dad was bringing to her; a sign of hope and connection, not just for herself but for Rubes as well.

'A singer, that's what you ought to be,' she repeated.

Ruby stood up. 'This is a daft game, Sara, you know it is. I think we should be getting back to Liam.'

They ran when they saw there was a crowd of people round him. The newsagent was there, talking into his mobile phone. He beckoned to Sara.

'Why did you leave him?' He wasn't accusing her, he wasn't making her feel guilty so she was able to answer.

'He'd got a bit better. We thought we'd get a coffee. What's happened?'

He didn't reply. He put his mobile carefully back into his jacket pocket and looked at her with those kind eyes. Sara's heart beat so strongly she felt faint and collapsed onto the pavement. People gathered from nowhere, as Ruby knelt down and held Sara in her arms. 'Come back, Sara, please come back.' A man from the crowd stepped forward but by now Sara was stirring. She looked up into the newsagent's face. He spoke quietly.

'The ambulance should be coming any minute.'

Ruby helped Sara up. 'We were going to take him home with us.'

'Too late, my dear. Now listen to me. It's better if you don't get muddled up with this. There's no knowing what will happen if you do.'

'But he's our friend, we can't just leave him.'

Sara intervened. 'I'm better now,' she pleaded with the newsagent but he was firm, treating them as if they were his daughters. 'I'll be here and I'll let you know what happens. I promise you that.' His voice was urgent. 'Just walk away for a bit. Otherwise you might not get home.'

Sara was crying so Ruby put her arm round her as they made their way out of the crowd.

'We shouldn't have been fooling around, we should have come back sooner, I've let him down again, Rubes.'

Ruby took out one of the pieces of screwed up tissue from her pocket and wiped Sara's eyes. 'There's nothing we can do at the moment,' she said, 'We'll go and watch the river go by. Come on, Sara, I thought you were the strong one.'

Sara went on crying. 'I told him he wouldn't be taken to hospital. I promised him.'

They wandered down to the river and leaned over the wall. Ruby held Sara's pale, cold hands.

'*You* haven't sent him to hospital. *They* have.'

'He'll get caught.'

'Sara, he's too ill to be caught. He scooped up everything there was in that tin. He's overdosed.'

Sara rubbed her hand up and down the side of her face. She caught her breath and looked terrified. 'Will he -?'

'We don't know, do we? All we do know is he's going to the best place.'

'I suppose so.' She wiped her nose on her sleeve. 'It was the shock. I never thought. Do you think he did it on purpose?'

'Who knows? He was pretty desperate. I don't think he saw a way out.'

Sara breathed deeply. 'He isn't the only one.'

'Yes, he is.' It was Ruby's turn to be strong. 'O yes, he is. We're going to start again, Sara, you and me. We're not going to go blazin' forever. One day it will be all good.'

Sara nodded, her eyes shining with tears. They were soothed by the tidal water flowing beneath them that carried sticks and debris and all the reflections of the sky. Sara held Ruby's arm and spoke quietly as if the words were for Ruby alone.

'Do you think there never was any hope for Liam and Dave?'

Ruby shook her head. 'There's always hope,' she said.

'Now *you've* changed.'

Ruby's liquid brown eyes were filled with warmth. 'Funny thing, Sara, it was you who helped me. Reminding me that I can get clean, that I can... well, yes, that I can sing.'

A passenger boat was passing and people waved. Ruby rose to the occasion and broke into song:

Where is love if it's rented out,
where is hope if it's full of doubt,
freedom's more than an open door,
there's no running any more.
You're my friend and I won't betray,
memories last till the end of day,
I won't leave like I did before,
there's no running any more.

Her voice warmed and lifted Sara. It brought back all the memories she had shared with Rubes, slowly raising her out of her grief and guilt. When Ruby reached the last few lines she turned and faced Sara and sang softly, for her this time, holding her hands, pulling her up from her grief.

But I've been running through the wind and rain,
going there and back again.
Don't go asking where I've roamed
' 'cos I've got no home.

They were silent for a while; then Sara gave Ruby a big hug. 'Thanks, Rubes. I'm all right now. Let's go back.'

Chapter seventeen

Freedom's more than an open door

The newsagent was closing shop, tidying shelves, making sure the refrigerator was shut tightly, dangling his bunch of keys.

'I'm glad you've come back. He's gone to Charing Cross Hospital. He's in good hands. Now listen, I have to get back home but if you ever need any help, I have a lot of connections up here. You'd be surprised how many people come into this shop and leave their cards or tell me their life story.'

'You sure Liam is all right?' said Sara, squinting up at the man's kindly eyes.

'I told you, he's in the best hands, that's all I can say. It's not just me. No-one can say more than that.'

He moved towards the door. 'I'm locking up now but maybe you'd like a coffee.'

Ruby looked at Sara and Sara imperceptibly nodded. 'We haven't any more money.'

The man smiled, 'It's all right, I'll raid the till.'

When they were settled in the coffee shop, the same one they had been to before, he told them his name was Tom and he had two children. He would have had three of course but Lucy had died.

Tell us about Lucy,' said Sara.

Tom sighed, 'She's... she was so like you,' he said, 'It's simple really. She got in with the wrong lot. We did all we could, you know. Liz – that's my wife- spent hours trying to sort her out, paying her attention, all the things mothers do.'

'Not mine,' said Ruby, 'I might as well not have been her daughter for all she cared.'

'I'm sorry to hear that,' said Tom. 'I can only say we tried to keep Lucy with us but her friends had more pull than we had. One night she ran off with them and we didn't know where she was. Can you believe it, we didn't know what had happened to her for six weeks. We looked everywhere, contacted no end of agencies, but no one could find her. In the end we had a phone call from a hospital. She'd been taken in the night before.'

He found it hard to speak now and Sara and Ruby waited quietly. Tom took out a large white tissue, blew his nose then spoke again, his voice weighted with grief.

'She was dead before we arrived. Overdose.'

He hastily sipped his coffee and looked at his watch. 'Funny thing, it was about this time we got up there. Queen Mary Hospital, Intensive Ward.'

'I'm so sorry,' said Ruby, 'and I see now why you understand what we're feeling. I'd also like to know if you're trying to tell us something.'

'I've seen it happen once,' he said, looking directly at Ruby, 'and I wouldn't like to see it happen to you. I've talked to other kids; sometimes they listen and sometimes they don't. It's what I do to try and make sense of Lucy's death. It's all I can do really.'

'Thank you,' said Sara, 'We are listening, aren't we, Rubes?'

Ruby sighed and spoke in a subdued voice. 'I don't know if I trust anyone.'

Tom smiled, 'That's just not true, you trust Sara, I can see that.'

'She blows hot and cold,' said Sara, 'A little while ago she said I made her feel different. Now she's making out she doesn't trust anyone.'

'Except you,' Ruby said warmly to Sara, 'but you've got to be careful.' She spoke as if Tom wasn't there.

'We live in a world of fear,' said Tom, 'and those who want to do good are often accused of all sorts of obscenities.' There was a streak of anger in his voice.

'I'm sorry,' said Ruby. 'Every one of my mum's blokes took her away from me. I know I'm nearly an adult, but I'm not that good with men. Except for Dave, and he was like me which is why he turned to drugs.' She looked long and hard at Tom. 'Yes, I do trust you. You've been good to us.'

'Ruby's going to be a singer,' Sara told Tom.

'Don't start that,' said Ruby.

Tom smiled. 'I think you will.'

'Why do you say that?'

'Once you're off drugs you'll want to move ahead.'

'I've nowhere to go,' said Rubes. 'Anyway my first thing is to find out about Dave.'

Tom felt in his pocket and brought out a sheet of paper. 'This might come in useful one day.'

'She's always getting pieces of paper,' said Sara.

'Angel messages,' said Ruby, in storytelling mode.

Tom smiled. 'It's a list of places where you can get help. It might come in useful.'

'I'll take it ,' said Sara as Tom stood up to say goodbye. 'I know Rubes. She'll lose it. And thank you, Tom, for all you have done. Before you go can you tell us how to get to Charing Cross Hospital?'

'We need his mother's address,' said the charge nurse to Sara. 'Do you know it?'

Sara nodded. 'She cared for him, you know. She was always giving him money.'

'Perhaps that was the problem,' replied the nurse, 'He needed help for his addiction, not money for it.'

She was a tall, commanding figure but spoke gently. 'Will you be able to get home?'

Sara nodded. 'That's not a problem. My mother will be arriving in about an hour to take us back.' She and Ruby stood silently for a moment, looking out of the window onto the busy road.

'It's a shock you know, even though you think it might happen.'

The nurse spoke quietly, 'Would you like to see him?'

Sara and Ruby looked at each other.

'You go,' said Ruby, 'I'll stay around. I'm no good at that sort of thing.'

Sara stood inside the blue curtains looking down at the white sheet that covered Liam. Only his head showed, those

143

green eyes shut tight never to open again. She thought she would be devastated but she wasn't. She knew he was at last in the place where he wanted to be and where in an unconscious way he had wanted to take her. All the things they had done together ran through her mind, all the choices she had made to be with him, and only a little while ago, though it seemed ages, the choice she had finally made to live, to make something of her life. She was too moved for tears, she knew she had to leave him; but she didn't know how. If it wasn't for the nurse coming quietly through the curtains she would have stood there all night.

'Your friend's waiting for you,' she said, 'Are you ready?'

'I don't know what to do.'

The nurse smiled sympathetically. 'Your friend is waiting. She tells me your mother's coming very soon.'

Sara nodded. She had almost forgotten. She took one last, long look at Liam and followed the nurse out into the reception area. It was only when she and Ruby were outside the hospital that she began to cry, thinking of her last sight of Liam, remembering Dad, who had not chosen to die. As she held Ruby's hand she could hear Dad's voice, soothing her, telling her how precious she was, how he understood why she had stood by Liam, how that loyalty would help her in life. And then she thought of Mum.

Sara shivered. It was cold waiting around in Waterloo Station and Ruby unzipped her jacket and put it round Sara's shoulders. 'It's shock. Shock makes you cold. Your mum won't be long.'

And amazingly there she was, running towards Sara, calling her name over and over again, embracing her, cupping her face, hugging her in a desperately joyful way. For a while Sara looked back at her mother in silence. *How grey your hair is, look, it's turned white in places. But your eyes are the same, straight and seeking.* There were many things Sara wanted to say but they were stuck deep down in herself; she had no voice that could express them.

Then her mother turned to Ruby and kissed her. 'It's so good to see you as well.'

Ruby had tears in her eyes, she couldn't remember the last time an adult had embraced her. She spoke in a shaky voice, 'Good to see you. It's been a hard day, Sara's had a real shock.'

'It's Liam,' said Sara in a scarcely audible voice, 'He's...he's dead.'

She watched her mother stiffen, as if she had been hit and could no longer speak; then she cradled Sara's hands and rubbed them as if to bring them back to life.

'I'm, I'm so sorry.'

Sara spoke in a hoarse whisper, 'You're not, you always wanted him to die.'

Her mother drew her into her arms. 'I'm sorry, I'm so sorry. You've had enough as it is.' After a while she let go of Sara and a heavy silence stood between them like a wall. When at last she spoke her voice was strained. 'We'd better get home, darling. Emily is longing to see you. I hope you will come and stay with us as well, Ruby.'

Ruby stood silent and Sara pleaded with her, 'Why don't you come with us?'

Ruby edged herself forward, held Sara's hands and spoke in a barely audible voice. 'Listen, Sara, I'd like to be in your family and I'm grateful to your mum, but like I said, I'm going to try to find Dave first. Like I told you, we bear the same scars.I think that lady will help me. Then I'll come. I promise you I'll come, Sara.'

'Are you sure that's wise?' said Sara's mum.

'It's the way I feel,' said Ruby, 'I don't know if that's wise or not.' She watched Sara's mum open her bag, get out her purse and take out some money.

'This is for you. If you get into any trouble phone straight away.'

'How can I thank you?'

'By coming back,' said Sara, 'as you said you would. Here's that phone number -' she took the creased-up note from her pocket. 'You know, that lady's number.' She scrunched it into Ruby's pocket. Then she felt in her own pocket again. 'What about this list Tom gave us?' She offered it to Ruby.

'You keep that, I'm bound to lose it. You know me.'

'Well, don't lose the other one.'

They held each other fast like two people who might drown without each other.

Chapter eighteen

I won't leave like I did before

It was early morning when Sara woke and recalled her dream. She was on the downs. It was a crisp, frosty, sunny winter's morning, bathed in a bright winter light that was everywhere. The hard sunlight nestled into the fir trees and lay along twigs like splinters of grass, so that the light seemed to be coming from the bare bones of the trees themselves. She was with the white horse, the one who was tethered on the downs. In her dream he was not an old work horse, but slim, young, already saddled for a ride. She untied him and lightly, painlessly, leapt onto his back. He might have had wings, he galloped so smoothly, so faultlessly, away and away. She was so taken up, her confidence so complete that she was wholly absorbed in this ride. There was nothing else in her dream but the movement of the horse and the bright winter light.

She looked wonderingly round the room. Was this the place the horse had brought her to? After a while she remembered where she was. She stared for a long time at the window. It was covered by crisp, blue curtains and the early daylight diffused through them, as if the outside world was the same light blue. She looked slowly round the room again. Her photographs were still on the chest of drawers in the corner, and she began to speak to the picture of her father about the nightmare she had had. For surely it had been a nightmare? Then the truth fell on her and tears trickled down her cheeks. She would never, never see Liam again.

She wiped away her tears and sat up. She pushed back the bed covers and went over to the corner chair where her ancient teddy bear was sitting. His stuffing was still showing through the holes, his one beady eye was hanging a quarter of an inch on a string, his nose was grey and spotted with black pencil marks.

She picked him up, took him back to bed and tried to re-arrange the eye. She couldn't help thinking of JoJo.

There was a scuffle on the landing and Sara hastily shoved her bear under the bedclothes. The door opened very slowly and Emily put her head round.

'Can't sleep. Can I come in?' She squeezed through the door, carefully shut it, ran over to Sara's bed and slid inside. 'It's ever so early. What's this lump?'

'Ted.'

'Why don't you let him sit up?'

Sara pulled out the bear and gave it to Emily. She pushed back her hair and looked straight up to the ceiling.

'I can't believe I'm back.'

Emily leaned over and pinched her arm. 'You feel real.' She sat up and fiddled with the fold of the sheet. 'Tell me what happened.'

'You wouldn't understand.' Sara lifted her arm and pointed to the ceiling. 'It was topsy turvy, like living up there, upside down.'

'We were so worried. Why didn't you come home?'

After a few minutes Sara said: 'I didn't know how to.'

Emily settled down again and for a while they lay in silence. 'What did you eat?'

'Porridge and stuff like that.'

'I hate porridge. Ben ate porridge.' Emily looked at her sister with news in her eyes. 'I think he was fed up because Mummy was always out looking for you.'

'How do you know?'

'He's not around any more.'

Sara closed her eyes. Mum had put her first before anyone. How could she have been so mistaken?

'What's the matter?' said Emily.

'I was just thinking. Where did Mum look?'

'She went up to London. I looked too, up on the downs. You know where our old white horse grazes, I was sure you were really there with him. I used to spend hours and hours waiting for you, but you never came.'

'Why did you think I was there?'

'I just did. I thought you were lying on the grass, somewhere. Then one day the horse wasn't there and I thought you'd gone off on him.'

'That would have been nice, going somewhere else just with a horse. Has he come back?'

Emily flopped back onto the pillow 'No he's never come back. I think there was something wrong with him and he was put down.'

Sara turned her head and looked at the photograph of her father. She became so silent and absorbed that Emily crept out of bed and tip-toed out of the room. Then she poked her head round the door.

'Did you miss me?'

'I used to wonder what you were doing.'

'I missed you all the time.'

Emily ran across the room and climbed back into bed with Sara. They hugged each other and lay together on their backs, arms entwined, looking at the ceiling.

'Did you have a toothbrush?'

'Sort of. I used my finger.'

'What about your hair, did you have a hair brush?' Emily pushed back her long fair plaits.

'No, but Rubes had a comb. Rubes always looked good.'

'Why hasn't she come back?'

'She's got things to do and then she is coming back. She's going to live with us. Do you mind?'

'No, I don't think so.'

Sara turned to her little sister. 'Do you believe in angels?'

'What do you mean believe in?'

'I don't know what I mean, it just seemed that every time we were right down in the pit somebody helped us out.'

'Oh, I see. You mean people.'

'Sort of.'

Sara pushed off the bedclothes and went over to the window. Last time she had seen the garden it was spring and, although so much had happened, it only seemed a minute ago. As if in a twinkle of a dream, the cycle of daffodils had been waved away and here were the summer roses glowing like brightly-coloured powder puffs; red, pink, yellow. The chestnut trees on the downs were vast green umbrellas, the hedgerows had knitted together and were overgrown with brambles. She turned back to Emily who was hugging the teddy bear. 'I'm going for a walk. Do you want to come?'

'I'm not dressed.'

'Nor am I. I'm going to put on my jacket.'

'I'm too sleepy. You won't go away again, will you?'

Sara bent over and kissed Emily. 'Promise you I won't, never again.' Emily relaxed and closed her eyes.

Sara put on her jacket and rummaged in the inside pocket. Tom's list was still there. She must put it somewhere safely. You never knew when you might need it.

As Sara crept out, there was no other sound in the house.

The sun was just over the horizon, red and slow. The grass was damp and she enjoyed the feeling of wetness squeezing over her feet. It was a mild, early morning, the magpies scraped and wheeled about a clump of trees and there seemed to Sara something unearthly about the light filtering through the branches. She walked towards the hut and peered through the window. The little things she and Liam had brought up to make it into a home had been taken away. Her imagination had filled the hut with so many memories; it had grown into a place that stretched out into everything that had happened to her and Liam and Ruby. In reality it was small and empty and the door was padlocked. It was a place she would never visit again.

Now the sun was rising in leaps, and as she wandered over to see if the white horse had really gone as Emily had said, a thrush sang in a tree and little brown meadow butterflies fluttered over the grass. The enclosure was empty, the grass grown high. She turned away but she didn't feel too sad. Everything was moving on and so must she and Ruby.

After a little while she went home. Emily was fast asleep in her bed and Sara slipped in beside her. She felt so contented to be next to Emily that for a minute she stopped thinking about all that had happened: she drifted off to sleep and had another vivid dream : She and the horse circled over a part of the downs that she never seen before; here was a great smooth slope, more like a huge lawn, that swept down to a little wood. They were forced to go more slowly in the wood, but the horse still galloped and she bent forward, fearlessly, to avoid the overhanging branches and twigs. The dark wood was speckled with light; a kaleidoscope of sun rays played on them as they went. Then, abruptly, the wood came to an end, and Sara found herself riding on a chalky mountain, overgrown with thistles and bright yellow dandelions. She turned the horse to go back through the wood, but the rows of trees had turned into a high stone wall. She knew it was the wall to her house, although it was twelve feet high and it stretched along for miles. She looked ahead. Another barren mountain rose abruptly in front of her, itself almost like a wall, and the passage in between the wall and the mountain was very narrow. Although it was not visible to her she knew the path overhung a precipice. She clung to the horse and he turned to the right and began to tread delicately, gently, along this narrow path. It became darker and darker and, at the point where she could barely see - for all the bright winter light had gone and there was only one dull star hanging in the sky above - she woke. Emily had gone and Mum was standing there with a tray of tea and biscuits. Sara rubbed her eyes and sat up.

For the next few days Sara did very little except ease the tiredness and depression out of her bones. One day Mum came into her bedroom and spoke excitedly. 'We've had a phone call, darling. Ruby is in a hostel and she's being looked after. The only thing is she mustn't be in touch with anyone for a month.'

'A whole month?'

Mum smiled. 'It will go quickly enough.'

Sara leapt out of bed and danced round the room. 'She's made it! Ruby's made it!'

It was impossible to tell anyone how happy she felt. Ruby had been on a long, long journey that only she understood. For days, half unconsciously, Sara had been willing Ruby to take the right steps and now it was as if a great burden had fallen off her shoulders. The next day she became so relaxed, she slept in the day and woke to find Emily sitting beside her reading a book. She had a sense of timelessness as if she was recuperating from a long illness.

Mum asked no questions, knowing there could be no replies. But she did tell her Ben's farmhouse was for sale and Ben had only just gone to Australia to live with his son. 'Things were going badly in England,' she said, 'and in the end he had to cut his losses.'

Sara looked quizzically at Mum. 'Did he hope to start a new life with you?'

'At one time I think he did, but he knew I wouldn't go.'

'I'm sorry, Mum.'

Mum smiled. 'Everything moves on.'

Slowly, very slowly, Sara found she was distancing herself from Liam and all that he stood for. She was surprised at herself; she didn't think she would ever, ever get over his death. But the less she felt about Liam, the more she thought about Rubes. Three weeks had passed, and although she knew Rubes was on a cure, she couldn't help wondering if she would ever see her friend again. She felt panic-stricken at the thought. It was then she decided to go and see Gran who was always comforting.

'On my own,' she told Emily, 'Don't forget I haven't seen Gran for ages.' She knew she would have to pass Ruby's house and she didn't want Emily to be there.

Of course it wasn't strictly Ruby's house. Her mum had only rented it and Sara wasn't too shocked to find it abandoned with a TO RENT sign attached to the gate. The garden was thick with ground elder, dandelions and thistles. The windows were dusty and silent. If only Ruby's mother was there she could tell her about Ruby. Then she pulled herself up. Ruby's mum had never cared, never. Sara lingered for a little while, remembering the last time she had passed - when Ruby had leaned out of the window and called down, and how they had stood around on the pavement and planned the party. She hurried on, hoping Ruby was staying the course.

To her great relief Gran hadn't changed at all. It seemed as if nothing had happened since the last time she had been here.

Gran looked the same, felt the same and no doubt would say the same things. Sara was astounded. While she had experienced so much and had hopefully changed, Gran had sat here through it all.

Sara pulled out the little stool and smiled at Gran, then turned away again.

Gran pulled a face. 'You look as if you don't know whether you're coming or going. Still, you're all in one piece. Even if you're as thin as a broomstick and your locks are all over the place.' Sara pushed her hair back behind her shoulders.

'Be a good girl, and make tea. I have a new mug that's blue with a band of red writing that says: What would I do without my Gran!'

Sara laughed and when the tea was ready she put Gran's mug on the little table beside her and sat down. Gran slowly stretched out her fingers and patted the back of Sara's hand. 'How are you feeling, dear?'

Sara laughed with embarrassment. 'All right, I suppose. But I'm really worried about Rubes. She's staying in London in a hostel and is meant to be getting off drugs. I'm hoping she's all right.'

Gran gave Sara one of her direct stares. 'It's hard not to know how someone you love is getting on. But you will. Ruby's hardier than you, Sara. She'll be all right.'

'I know but I'm worried.'

Gran laughed and finished off her tea. 'Everything takes time. Look at me, four score and twenty, and I still haven't learned not to worry.' Gran stretched out both her bent hands and placed them over Sara's and looked straight into her grand-daughters eyes. 'You needs building up, Sara, but, if you're willing, God's on your side. You know that, in your heart of hearts. And so does Rubes.'

Sara laughed. 'You wouldn't believe it, Gran. Rubes believes in angels.'

'She's got to believe in something or she'd be right down the pan. Don't you worry about her, Sara. If she has her angels she's all right. Now would you pour me out another mug of tea, dear.'

Gran sipped her tea steadily, then went on firmly. 'You and Rubes will be all right as long as you put things behind you and make sure you make the most of what you have. I'm sure that's what you'll both do. What's the time, dear?'

'Quarter past six.'

'Tele time. There's something to look forward to.'

Gran slowly placed her television glasses on her nose. This familiar incongruous sight comforted Sara. She settled down on the stool and watched the tele, somehow protected by Gran's straightforward concentration.

When she left the house she went back over the downs. She walked on until Gran's house was out of sight, then she sat herself down in the long grass, put her head on her knees and cried and cried, partly for Liam, and partly for reasons she didn't understand. She wiped her eyes on the sleeve of her shirt, then lay down in the grass and watched a lark circle round and round in the blue sky. Suddenly it dived, but she didn't see where. Instead, her eyes closed and her mind was overwhelmed by a slow, heavy desire to sleep. So she slept for an hour and when she woke up she felt refreshed. She brushed off some of the countless seeds that covered her clothes and watched them spray down to the ground. They wouldn't all grow, she knew that, but many of them would shoot up and unknowingly add to next year's grass. That's how it should be for everyone, she thought.

Several days later Mum took Emily out with her friend to visit the donkey sanctuary. She wanted Sara to go with them but Sara felt like staying around, taking it easy. She wasn't even up when the phone rang. She nearly didn't answer it but the ringing was so persistent she got out of bed and ran downstairs.

'Hi, Sara.'

'Rubes! Rubes!It's been ages.'

'Can I reverse the charge?'

' Of course you can.'

Sara's heart was in her mouth. 'Tell me everything, I want to know everything - from when I left for home.'

Sara could tell Rubes was smiling. ' It's so good to hear your voice, Sara. I'll tell you the story of everything. OK? Then maybe you will come and visit me. It hasn't been easy. Once I bunked off with this guy who said he knew Dave. It was a load of rubbish so I went back. They weren't even cross with me.'

Ruby had a lot to say and after the phone call, Sara climbed over the little wall at the back of their garden and stretched out under the great oak tree where she used to wait for Liam. Now she thought about no-one but Rubes. She felt so close to her she could see her eyes, feel her skin, watch her full-hearted expressions and above all, hear her voice in her head, just as it was on the phone. In reality she had interrupted Rubes many times, especially at the end of the call when she pleaded with her never to run away again. But now it wasn't like that. Lying down under the tree she could only hear Rubes telling her the story of what had happened.

Chapter nineteen

Your heart says it's enough

'You know what I am, Sara, not shy, but frightened of change.
I've had too much of it, you know, what with all those boyfriends
Mum had. The thing was, I didn't want to get in touch with
that lady straight away; I needed to be on my own to face
whatever happened to Dave. She would have been smiley but not
understood what I was about. Anyway, I thought the best thing
was to get back to the squat because I might pick up a clue there,
see? After all it was the last place I saw Dave, wasn't it? It was
your Mum's money that got me there so thank her again, won't
you? It was late but not difficult to find the trains and I knew
where to get off and all that. But what do you think happened?
When I got to the squat it was all locked up, The Fuzz must have
been back, that was for sure. I wondered if anyone had gone
round the alley way like we used to– getting through a window
or something. Anyway, that's what I did. I couldn't see, but I
still remembered all those yellow and red shapes looping their
way under the windows. I managed to push open the back door
which had already been forced by someone else and went down
the corridor and into the big room – you remember it. I felt as if
I was being quite brave, but I wasn't really, I was driven on by the
thought of Dave. I know you understand that.

I wish you'd been with me, Sara. First of all the room was
just like it used to be. An oil lamp was lit in the corner and threw
off this soft, yellow light over half the room - those red curtains
and that torn print, they were still there. Those curtains were
almost drawn so everything was dark just like it used to be. And
then I saw some guys lounging around on those filthy old chairs,
and I thought I saw Dave sitting cross-legged on the sofa like
he always used to with his lovely black curly hair bushing out

over his shoulders. But it wasn't him, I guess one druggy looks
like another. Then I saw another guy sitting on the mattress
wearing clothes I'd seen before. I could have sworn it was Steve
but it wasn't. You know me, Sara, hooked by the sight of it all,
and when I went into that squat it seemed like the place to be.
You know how I forget things– well, at that moment I didn't
remember any of the stuff we'd said about singing and that; I just
wanted to forget everything. You're the only person who really
understands this. Well, there was a tin of blue tabs down there
on the floor behind the sofa, and I just took some and stuffed
them in my mouth before they could stop me. I can't remember
much about that session – I think I must have knocked myself
right out. Anyway, when I came to I didn't know where I was or
what time it was or anything, in fact I felt really ill. Afterwards
I realised these squatters had been quite worried about me. I
mean, they didn't want a body on their hands, did they? I don't
know how long it was before I asked them if they knew Dave or
Si – that's why I've come, I told them, to find out about them.
It turned out they did know about Si. They said he was in the
nick and probably all the others were as well, and that's where I
should be and I couldn't stay with them, so I better get a move
on. Then they went silent on me and just stared at me like the
medusa or something, trying to turn me to stone. But it wasn't
so much them that overwhelmed me. It was the silence I felt
inside me. If you'd been there it wouldn't have been like that, I'd
have been sparky, I know I would. Instead - I was so ashamed,
Sara, you wouldn't believe it- I began to cry. Those guys were so
unfriendly or maybe so angry because I'd taken their precious
blue tabs that in the end they forced me out of the room, half
carried me down the corridor past the kitchen and out of the
back door. I shouted and screamed at them but they weren't
having any. Talk about freezing me out. Well, I staggered down
the alley way and collapsed at the end of it. You see, I was really
ill. Then he came along, this nice guy with his little girl, and
I told him I needed to make a phone call and he took out his
mobile and smiled at me. 'Here's the number,' I said, getting it
from my pocket. I left it completely to him, I felt that ill. Looking

back I think he was another angel in disguise.'

Sara closed her eyes and drifted into a light sleep. Now. instead of hearing Ruby, it was as if, in her dream-like state, she saw all that was happening to her friend.

The hostel was bright and cheerful and Ruby had a room to herself. She lay in bed, looking round. The walls were painted soft lilac and round them hung pictures of animals with their young. In one picture there was a little white bear standing between the huge paws of its mother, in another a gorilla hugging its baby in its arms, and in another an elephant following the tail of its huge mother. Ruby liked the baby elephant best, it looked as if it was going somewhere. She stared at the pictures for a long time, trying to remember how she got here. She only had a vague memory of being in a car and driving through London. She remembered a lady was at the wheel and from time to time she talked to her kindly. Ruby learned she was called Mrs Bearman but everyone called her Rose. She said she didn't always drop notes in buskers' hats but she was very taken with Ruby's voice, and maybe her sister who was a singer, could help her when she was better. That is all she could remember.

The door creaked open and there was Rose standing with a bunch of roses in her hand. 'I picked them out of the garden. Smell them, their scent is beautiful.' She gave the roses to Ruby and looked around for a vase. There was a green glass one on the windowsill and she filled it with water from the cold tap in the sink that stood opposite the bed.

'I've never had flowers before,' said Ruby, ' not even from Dave.' She handed Rose the flowers. 'Do you know where Dave is?'

Rose carefully arranged the pink blossoms.

'It's not what I'm here for,' she said, 'but one of the patients might know.'

'I still miss him,' said Ruby.

Rose drew up a wooden chair and sat by the bed.

'Rest, then recovery,' she said, 'That's what we're about. The roses are part of it, of course.'

159

She was silent for a while and then directed her gaze straight at Ruby - she had the sort of blue eyes that you trusted. 'You were taking big risks, my girl, and you mustn't do that again. Now what about your relations? We have to tell them where you are.'

Ruby slid up the bed and pushed her back against the pillow. 'I haven't got any. I've never known my Dad and I've no idea where my Mum is. She left me, see?'

Rose shook her head and drew her fingers through her short curly grey hair. 'I'm sorry to hear that. Have you a friend?'

Ruby's eyes glowed warm and she smiled, 'Oh yes, she's called Sara Martin and she's gone home to her Mum's. I've got the phone number in my head if you want it.'

Rose took out a pen and a notebook from her black bag. 'That would be a good idea.' When she had written the number down she put the notebook back in her bag.

'Now listen to me, Ruby. That all lies in the past and we must occupy ourselves with the present and the future. You have great promise but you must totally give up your present life if you're going to fulfil yourself. If you are willing to go by our rules, you'll get better, there's no doubt about it.'

'What rules?'

'It's quite tough but I think you can do it. You must stay here for a month without seeing or talking to anyone from outside. You must be willing to listen to what we have to say and we will help you to give up drugs.'

'Say I run away?'

'You have three chances to come back and then that's it. After three goes I'm afraid we have to close the door. I would never want that to happen to you.'

Ruby stared hard at the roses. 'No-one has ever given me a bunch of flowers before.'

The first week went well. Rose kept an eye on her, talked to her, gave her substitutes to help her withdrawal and Rubes was enchanted by all the attention she was getting. She would do anything, anything at all for Rose. Rose encouraged her to sing to the others while they were making pots and rugs and purses. Then Rubes decided to make a bedside mat for Sara. It would be blue and white and small and warm so Sara would never have to go to bed with cold feet. It was difficult at first, but she persisted and was half way through when she met this guy Jim who knew Dave. Jim was a middle-aged man with a bald head and scars all over his face and arms. He often wore a wide hat, even indoors, that made him look like a gangster. He came in a week after Ruby and was hoping for a cure in a few days.

'That won't happen,' said Ruby, 'it takes ages.'

'Can't stay around for ages,' said Jim, 'Got me mates to think of. One of them's only just come out of the can.'

'Who's that?'

'My mate Dave.'

'Dave Hanks?'

'You bet.'

'He's my mate too.'

Jim took off his hat and scratched his bald head. 'Come with me, we'll find him together.'

Ruby kept thinking of Rose who had been so good to her and was arranging for her to meet her sister. But wasn't Dave more important? Wasn't this a chance to sort it all out?

'O K.'

'This place stinks,' said Jim, 'I'm not hanging around here. I'm bunking off tonight. Dave should be around.'

'Where?'

Jim shrugged his shoulders. 'He'll be around.'

They were not locked in, although outside the door was secured and you had to ring the bell to get into the hostel. They escaped just after supper when everyone was in the dining room. They took the Underground to Piccadilly and Jim soon came across his mates huddled together in an alley way, stashing dope into their satchels. They were making for a safe house, they said, there was this squat that hadn't been raided, just down the line. Ruby hung around, but Jim seemed to have forgotten all about her and Dave. He was deep in conversation with another older man, laughing and putting his arm round his shoulder. They moved off, and Ruby got talking to a tall, thin girl called Rachel who was walking beside her. 'I can tell you about Dave,' she said, when Ruby asked her. 'His girlfriend was Katie who was my friend.'

Ruby looked angry. 'If you must know, I'm his girlfriend. Tell me what happened.'

' Dave and Katie were on the run. She told me later he was going to Cornwall, but he didn't want her to go with him. He'd be safer on his own, he said, and he left my friend behind, just like that. I reckon he was pretty shifty. Come on, we'd better catch up with the others.'

The girl hurried on and looked back. 'Aren't you coming?' she shouted.

Ruby turned her back silently and walked the other way. She was so angry with Dave she couldn't speak. She took the Underground back to the hostel and knocked on the door.

Chapter twenty

Without words

A few weeks later

Ruby was wearing high-heeled sandals that revealed her toenails. They were painted vermilion red and looked like bright shells on the end of her feet. Her top was purple and her jeans slim. Good old Rubes, thought Sara, she's just the same. But when she took a closer look at her friend's face she thought it looked more grown – up, or was it simply that her curly black hair was held back by a pink band and her forehead was clear?

They looked at each other for a long time – there were no words for this moment, it was too intense, too fragile, as if everything might be different now that everything else *was* different. It was only when Ruby laughed, that warm, glowing, infectious laugh, that Sara knew it was going to be all right.

'So you made it!'

'Did you doubt it?'

'Yes, I did.'

They were sitting on a bench in the garden of the hostel. It was overgrown with wild grasses and bushes that had not been tended. Someone had once taken an interest in a dried-up vegetable patch where tomatoes were hanging ripe and full from hairy green stalks. They felt at ease in the hostel's unkempt garden, it was untouched, unmonitored, no-one was trying to change it.

Ruby laughed. 'Well, you're wrong. Rose has fixed up something really good for me.'

Sara's heart sank. 'You mean you won't be coming home?'

Ruby leaned over and hugged Sara. 'Of course I'm coming home, you great fizzie, and I want to see what's happened to that place I used to live in; I bet someone else is there now. I bet my mum never left an address or anything.'

Sara took Ruby's hands and lifted them up and placed them on hers, so they were palm to palm. 'Look, your mum may have gone away, and you may not feel very happy about my mum because she's neat and everything; but it is home and I'm there and we want you to always think of it as home. I know it's complicated when it's *not* your home, but do you see what I mean? And I'm sorry I keep saying the word "home".'

They stayed palm to palm while they were talking as if the gesture reinforced everything they said.

'You daft thing,' said Ruby, 'I really do like your mum. I tell you something, I wish my mum had been like yours.'

'You don't?'

'I do.'

There was a little silence between them.

'- And I wish I had a sister like you have,' went on Ruby, 'She's small and cute with those fair plaits of hers, and I'd like to dress her up and play fairy queens with her.'

'Sorry to tell you she's not the fairy queen type. She's sort of straightforward.'

'I know but you can have straightforward fairy queens,' said Ruby.

They dropped their hands and laughed and relaxed into silence. After a while the sun shone straight into their eyes and the garden was transformed into a desert of golden grass. Even the tomatoes hung burnished.

'It's beautiful here,' said Sara.

'Mostly it's not.' Ruby pulled a face. 'But I've been lucky. Rose has been an angel, and this is the really good news I have to tell you.'

She glanced purposefully at Sara. 'She has this sister who used to sing in opera. Well, this sister who's called Mariana came up one day to hear me sing. She was so impressed she said she was willing to take me on and let me repay her later. But the best bit of news is –'

'It can't get better than that,' said Sara, shielding her eyes from the sun.

Ruby laughed. 'Oh yes it does. You see, she doesn't live far away from where we live. She lives in Brighton.'

'Brighton! I can't believe it. That's where I'm going to college! Mum and I fixed it up last week. I'm going to do a Foundation Course.'

They leapt up and danced round the wild garden together as if they knew this elation would never last but would never be forgotten. They tripped up the tomato plants and snagged their jeans on thorn bushes.

'Hey, do you remember? shouted Sara, twirling round. 'Do you remember how we danced when we were ten?'

'I've got an elephant's memory,' said Ruby, leaping over a bush. 'I've never forgotten it. I had that gold bracelet from Mum and I wore it every day, do you remember? That was when we danced together.'

She took a huge leap across the vegetable patch with Sara behind. 'I kept it round my wrist until Mum left for the second time. Then I dumped it in someone's garden. Tell you something,' she went on, pirouetting across the grass, 'I don't care any more about that tore-up bracelet. It was off a lorry, anyway. I suddenly don't care.'

Now they held hands and swung round and round until they were so dizzy they subsided onto the grass, flat out, side by side, trying to catch their breath again. The sun had just tipped over the roof of the hostel and arrowed down to where they lay. They both shut their eyes to the sharp light. Ruby spoke first. 'What about that time we danced when you got that prize for drawing. Do you remember?'

Sara shielded her eyes as she smiled. 'It was the only prize I ever got. We danced all over the playground and they told us off for getting in the way of other children. We didn't take any notice, did we? We were top of the tree! Anyway, we weren't in the way, were we?'

'Yes, we were. We were just too excited to care.'

Sara opened her eyes and held up her hand to shield her eyes. 'We danced together even though it was me that got the prize. It's the same with your singing.'

Ruby laughed. 'It's called reflected glory, but why not? '

Sara was silent for a moment wondering whether this was a good thing or a bad thing. Surely it was a good thing, crying when your friend was crying, laughing when your friend was laughing? Or could you be too close to someone? Were you bound to get disappointed at some time or other?

'We'll always be like that,' said Ruby, 'whatever happens.'

Sara leant up on one elbow. 'Hope so, Rubes. Now tell me, what was it like here?'

Ruby shrugged her shoulders. 'It depends who you are, know what I mean? Some people couldn't stick it and just ran away. Rose said it was a good thing I was a young chick. It makes all the difference, she said, you can change when you're young but it gets harder- and if you're a peach cobbler you've had it.'

Sara laughed. 'That's a good one. Anyway, Rubes, I don't believe what you're saying. It must depend on who you are, not just your age.'

'Well, that's what she said, anyway, and it seems like it was true. As you know I did run away once, but when I knew the score I went back.'

Sara spoke quietly. 'Dave wasn't what you thought?'

Ruby sat up and brushed the grass off her hair. 'You can say that again. One look at another bird and he'd be off. He's always been like it, but I used to think –' her voice deepened – 'he couldn't resist me.'

Sara laughed. 'You couldn't be doing with him now, anyway. You're going to meet this fabulous male opera singer –'

'And he's going to seduce me with his tenor voice and give me all his cash money-'

'And you're going to have a house surrounded by apple trees and pear trees-'

'Come off it, I don't like apples or pears. I'm an orange person.'

'Then he's going to take you to Spain and you're going to live in a little house filled with the scent of orange blossom, and orange trees will line the roads.'

Angry voices from an open window of the hostel broke up their romantic story. Ruby stood up and pulled Sara to her feet. 'There's always a lot of noise round, it's hard to get away. When are they coming back?'

'About half an hour. Mum thought we would like time together while she's taking Emily to the kennels to get her-'

'A rescue dog?'

'That's it. Then we're all going back together.'

'She's not daft, your mum.'

'She tries.'

The angry voices drifted away and they began to stroll round the garden, slowly examining the wild poppies that stood by the fence like fragile red flags.

'I'm trying not to think opium,' said Ruby.

Sara laughed, 'Liam once thought he could make his own. He was out of his mind.'

They paused, looking at each other.

'How do you feel about him?'

'Sad, but I did something that helped me. I knew where he'd be buried so I went there to say goodbye. That made a difference, I think.'

They had come back to the bench and sat down on it. 'Tell me all about it,' said Ruby, once more lifting her face to the sun.

'Not much to tell really,' said Sara, shutting her eyes and following her memories.

'I knew I would have to say goodbye to him one day. You know, Rubes, no-one asked me to the funeral or let me know where he was buried.'

'Typical,' said Ruby and held Sara's hand.

'You're right there. I was wiped out like that, like a fly or something squashed underfoot. But the thing was I knew where he was going to be buried, I even remembered the words he said when we were running away. *I'm going to be buried here. I told my mum that the other day. It's the peace and quiet.*'

Ruby spoke to the sky. 'I suppose that shocked you when he said that?'

'It didn't feel like it at the time, but it must have done, else I wouldn't have remembered it, would I? Anyway, I decided to go back and retrace my footsteps. It felt like being on a pilgrimage, step by step walking where he had walked, a sort of memory pilgrimage which might make everything easier. In the end I did the journey several times, and at the finish I did feel better. Do you know, Rubes, it took four goes for me to – how can I put it? – to feel settled.'

'So where did you go?'

She sat back and listened to Sara's account of her first visit.

'I couldn't do this pilgrimage thing straight away. For a long time I was so tired it felt like an illness – know what I mean, Rubes? Then these little stirrings of energy nudged me inside somewhere and I decided to go and find Liam's grave. I thought about it for a long time and decided I wanted to approach the churchyard from the hill – you know, where me and Liam had slept out that night, right at the beginning.' She paused for a while, thinking about that moment.

'Go on,' said Ruby, 'Tell it like a story.'

' You and your stories. Well, I climbed nearly to the top of the hill and stopped to look at the pinewood in front of me. Even on that day, even in the sunlight, it still looked impenetrable, sort of black with shadows and something more ominous that I can't put my finger on. Do you remember those books we used to read, Rubes? Witches on broomsticks, Hansel and Gretal lost under the trees, the thunder of horses' hooves. They all raced through my mind but it wasn't really any of those things that made me feel uneasy. It was perhaps because, looking back at what had happened, the wood, seemed like a false refuge, a wrong turning. Of course I didn't know it when I went with Liam. All I thought was that I'd betrayed him, and the least I could do was to go along with him and that he was there, next to me, close as we are.

It was strange, as I stood there looking at the wood I reached out as if it was still possible to touch him, but there was no-one there, only a red admiral butterfly that went zigzagging from one of my arms to the other.'

'Perhaps Liam had turned into a butterfly,' interrupted Ruby with a grin, 'You never know.'

Sara smiled. 'It felt like that. It was then I retraced my footsteps – it seemed important to do that. I went slowly down the hill and over the road. The churchyard was behind a low wall, a little way from the church. Then another strange thing happened to me. I could hear Liam's voice whispering in my ears, the same words as before - it was like a record. *"I'm going to be buried here. I told my mum that the other day. It's the peace and quiet."'*

Sara turned to Ruby. 'If only you'd been there. I suddenly felt so alone, I can't tell you. I was looking for Liam's grave but my eyes were blurred. I wasn't crying or anything; I was just, well, unable to bear it. Then I found these new graves. His was by the fence that separated the graveyard from the allotments. There was one jam jar full of dead roses resting against a small white stone that was engraved with the words:

OUR BELOVED SON.

Our, why our? His father hated him and so did his brother. It should have read MY BELOVED SON. But I suppose that wouldn't have done.'

'The done thing,' said Ruby sitting upright. 'That's what everyone expects. The done thing. That's why we went wrong, come to think of it. It wasn't the done thing to fall in love with Dave or Liam.'

Sara said nothing for a while, then spoke quietly as if she was speaking a secret. 'Do you know, Rubes, I thought about love when I was standing by Liam's grave. I was under his influence, there was no doubt about that, and felt it was right for me to help him out after what I'd done. But - love, I'm not so sure. Tell you what Rubes, I'm no longer certain what, being in love is. I thought I was, you see, but now I think it was lots of other things that made me follow him.'

'Like needing to get away?' said Rubes.

Sara nodded. She remembered her feelings of constraint, as if she was bound by some sort of rope. She had never felt like that when Dad was alive.

'That was just one of the things. Guilt too, I always knew that. But there was something else I hadn't even thought about until I stood there looking down at the words and at the jam jar filled with dead roses. Promise you won't say anything?'

Ruby gave her a big hug. "'course I won't, you fizzie,' and she lifted up her palm and put it against Sara's. 'The sacred sign,' she said half humorously and began to quietly sing the verse from their song.

Palm to palm we were as one,
without words we'd just begun,
my soul's hungry, my soul is raw,
there's no running any more.

'Well, here it is then,' said Sara. 'I've hardly accepted it myself, but I think this is the real reason why I ran away. Not the guilt, not the love, not the sex, nothing like that. It was something quite different. Do you know what, Rubes? I think I went looking for my Dad.'

Ruby said nothing for a while and then spoke slowly.

'Some people would think that's daft but then they don't know what it's like. I think when something has happened to one of your parents you're always looking for him.'

'You mean you're looking for your dad?'

'Not consciously, but there's a sort of absence in here.' Ruby pointed to her heart. 'It's deeper than Dave, and it's much deeper than Mum who's a cow and doesn't care anyway. But in my mind I've got this dad who does care.' She laughed. 'He's a singer too.'

'You bet,' said Sara, 'Does he play the cornet?'

'If you say so. He's there, even though I've never seen him and never will. Did you know he's an African Prince? He comes from Botswana and spends all his money on poor people.'

'They say day-dreaming doesn't do any harm.'

Ruby laughed. 'I just want you to know I understand about your search.'

They laughed and sat back. 'I knew you would, Rubes.'

They both looked up at the blue sky as it washed over them.

'It's a beautiful blue,' said Sara.

'Can you hear the birds?' said Ruby.

'You bet I can.'

'That means neither of us are too far gone. Now tell me more about being by Liam's grave.'

'I'll tell you about the last time, when I began to feel different. It was in the churchyard, and this time I went round looking at all the graves. I read the inscriptions - some were two hundred years old and almost unreadable. The messages were not in the same words but they mostly had the same meaning. It was only then I really discovered that loss was not a new thing, it was all around me.' Sara smiled. 'After a while I began to feel much more peaceful. Liam wasn't alone, he was part of something else now, and I could move on. That's when I decided to go to college, there, in the graveyard.' She looked straight at Ruby.

'Amazing, isn't it?'

'No! You'd come to the end of the pilgrimage and that's what you found.'

'It doesn't sound much,' said Sara.

'It sounds a lot to me,' said Ruby. A bell rang from inside the building and she stood up.

'Tea time. Let's go in. The others will be back soon.'

They walked through the sun-soaked grass where several painted lady butterflies were fluttering up and down and the tomato plants were bent over with golden fruit.

Other books by Susan Holliday

RIDING THE STORM

THE DREAM CAVE

THE TIME STREET GANG

and

THE RAG AND BONE BOY

Susan Holliday writing as Susan Skinner

SYMBOLS OF THE SOUL

Poetry

OUT OF NOWHERE

Susan has always enjoyed writing, illustrating and performing. As she needed to earn a living, a classroom seemed to be the ideal place in which to do all these things, so she became a teacher.

A little later she married and had three children, all of whom needed stories. Then, when her sister died, Susan and her husband inherited another four children. At this point there was a necessary gap in her creative work. All was not lost however. A few years later she was invited to go on the quiz show Busman's Holiday. It was then Susan introduced herself to millions as a poet! She has never looked back.

Susan has won numerous prizes for her poetry including the Julia Cairns first prize for poetry (Society of Women Writers) four times, the Kent & Sussex Poetry Society first prize and third prize in an Open University Shakespeare Society sonnet competition. Her poems and articles have appeared in a number of magazines and anthologies including Outposts, Envoi, Acumen, Weyfarers Childrens' Magazine.

She particularly enjoys writing books for young people and is also an artist and illustrator.

Some of her books are written under the name Susan Skinner.